For Sue, Shira & Dina

to Ava--

CAPER GETS EVEN!

A Shaggy Dog Story

by James Gelsey

Keep on Reading!

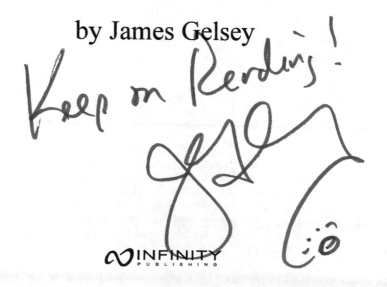

∞INFINITY
PUBLISHING

Copyright © 2011 by James Gelsey

ISBN 0-7414-6668-6

Printed in the United States of America

Published September 2011

INFINITY PUBLISHING
1094 New DeHaven Street, Suite 100
West Conshohocken, PA 19428-2713
Toll-free (877) BUY BOOK
Local Phone (610) 941-9999
Fax (610) 941-9959
Info@buybooksontheweb.com
www.buybooksontheweb.com

SUNDAY

So let's rewind things to last Sunday when my Aunt Connie came over to hang out with me and my six year old sister, Lizzie, a.k.a. "The Lizard." My parents were at a luncheon for someone my mom knows through her second cousin's aunt's grandmother or something. The Lizard was up in her room playing with those stupid microscopic dolls with the rubber clothes, and my aunt and I were in the family room looking through some old family pictures that she had brought over.

One of the pictures fell on the floor and I picked it up. It was a picture of my parents when they were a lot younger. My dad's beard was brown instead of mostly gray with a little bit of brown like it is now. And he was a lot skinnier too. My mom had way too much hair to ignore, and those glasses—what was she thinking?

The trees behind them were bare, and everyone in the background was wearing sweaters and scarves. My dad was holding a medium-sized whitish dog in his arms. It was one of those "mop dogs" with thick cords of fur dangling off its body. I asked my aunt about it and she got a weird look on her face, like someone thumped her on the back with a two-by-four. She blinked a couple of times, gave the picture a real quick glance, and then went back to categorizing the pictures. I asked her again.

Without looking up at me she said, "Oh, I don't know. Some dog your parents were watching for some friends who were out of the country, I think. Your father's always loved animals. I remember one time when we were kids he brought home a squirrel whose tail he said he'd accidentally run over on his bicycle. Don't ask me how he managed that."

I got the sense that she was just trying to distract me from the dog in the picture. The more I looked at it, the more I noticed how happy my parents seemed. My dad's eyes really sparkled in the sunlight, and my mom's whole face seemed to glow with this weird energy. Even the mystery dog looked happy, his pink tongue poking through the curtain of fur. And that's what made me want to find out more: there was something about that dog.

"You didn't answer my question," I said. "What's with the dog?"

Maybe it was the way I asked the question. Maybe it was the look on my face. Or maybe it was because Aunt Connie knows me so well that she realized that she'd never get a minute's peace unless she answered me. You see, my Aunt Connie and I go way back to...well, I guess to when I was born. She was the first person my folks let baby-sit me. That was when she was out of work so she visited a lot. Of course, I don't remember all this, but I know from the stories and the pictures.

Anyway, Aunt Connie took a deep breath—I mean, a really deep breath—and put the box of pictures on the floor.

"You, nephew of mine, are that dog's namesake," she said.

I quickly flipped through my brain's internal dictionary for the word. Namesake. Namesake. Something to do with a name. But what? Aunt Connie probably saw the confusion on my face and decided to clarify things.

"You know where your parents lived before you were born, right?" she asked.

"Hoboken," I nodded. My parents always talked about Hoboken like it was some magical, far away land. I visited it with them once. A lot of cars, everything close together. Definitely nothing magical about it.

"I used to take the bus from Manhattan once or twice a month for lunch or dinner or just to hang out with them," she said. "So the winter before you were born, I went out there and got to their building and rang the buzzer downstairs and climbed the four flights of steps and knocked. Your father opened the door a crack and a bolt of white fur shot out of the apartment and raced around my legs, I don't know, twenty times. Your father laughed and laughed. He bent down and swooped up the furry thing. He lifted the dog's face up to mine and said, 'Say hello, Caper.'"

At that point, Aunt Connie stopped talking and bit her lower lip.

"Caper, do you understand what I just told you?"

I nodded, but only because I thought she wanted me too.

"That winter there was this one mega-snowfall in March. The snow came up to my thighs. So you can imagine how hard it was for a lot of people, much less little dogs, to get around. Everyone was cooped up for three days, and that dog needed to run in a serious way. But when your father took him downstairs to go out after that snowfall, the dog bolted out the front door, slid on a patch of ice, and skidded out into the street where he..."

"What happened?" I asked.

"A snow plow came by and sort of scooped him up with the snow and pushed him into an enormous snow drift," Aunt Connie said. "Your father dug him out and rushed him to the vet, but it was too late. Poor thing didn't stand a chance against that plow."

I slowly nodded and made my best "Yes, yes, I understand, that's awfully sad" face. But I really didn't think it was sad. In

4

my head it became a cartoon with a snow plow launching the mop-dog hundreds of miles through the air until it landed in Alaska with a plop.

Aunt Connie turned away and wiped her right eye. I learned when I was little that she could only cry with her right eye. For some reason, her left eye couldn't make tears, which I used to think meant that the left side of her face couldn't feel sad. I called her right eye her crying eye.

"A few months later your folks found the house here," she said. "And that November you were born." She looked at me some more and sighed. "I know I'm going to pay for this, but I may as well tell you everything. In that picture, your parents knew your mom was pregnant with you. Later on, they bragged that they already had your name picked out. But after you were born, they changed their mind and decided to go with Caper."

Up to this point, I didn't really give it much thought, or even believe her. But then Aunt Connie's smile dissolved into her "I'm serious now" gaze.

"Caper, you have to promise me something," she said. Her voice sounded a little funny, like someone was pinching it as it came out of her mouth. "I'm sure if your parents wanted you to know this, they would have told you already. They haven't told you already, have they?"

I shook my head.

"I'm sorry, Caper," Aunt Connie continued. "I'm sure they will tell you one day, but until they do, you have to promise not to tell them that I told you."

I measured her words and what she wanted me to do. I certainly didn't want to get her in trouble with my parents. After all, she told me something about me that they never did. On the other hand, how could they *not* tell me something like that?

"Please, Caper, you have to double triple quadruple million times promise not say anything about this," Aunt Connie begged. "Your parents will be super mad at me if they find out." I think she was beginning to get desperate.

"Okay," I said as casually as I could. I didn't want Aunt Connie to feel any worse than she already did. And I certainly didn't want her to get in trouble on my account. After all, it wasn't her fault my parents never told me the truth about where my name really came from. I mean, all this time I thought I was named after Mom's Great Uncle Charlie. So I didn't say anything else about it, not even when my folks came home. I could tell Aunt Connie was a little nervous, but I kept my promise to her.

That night, I went online so my best friend Jonny and I could I.M. I told him what my Aunt Connie told me. His first reaction was, *cool!!!* Then he sent a second I.M. that changed everything: *so what's ur plan?*

Plan? Why did I need a plan? And then it all started to sink in. My parents had named me after a dog. A DOG! This was something that you didn't just shake off like a mosquito bite. This cut to the very heart of my identity!

The image of that dog haunted me all night. I even had a dream about it going to school in my clothes while I stayed home, locked in the closet wearing a dog collar. When my parents opened the closet door, they called me "Butchie." Lizzie stood there calling, "Here, puppypuppypuppy." And Serena Kingsley—this girl in my class—was there too, but I don't remember what she called me because I was too busy clawing at the dog collar.

The next morning I woke up panting and all sweaty. My mother said it was because my blood sugar went wacky during the night. But I knew the real reason: it was that little white dog. That twisted little mutt stole my parents' heart before I was born and laughed at me from the snow-plowed grave he's lying in.

In that moment I made up my mind. The only way to free myself from that canine horror was to get even with my parents for naming me after that stupid dog!

Jonny was right. All I needed was a plan.

MONDAY

All of my school days start the same way. My mom wakes me up two or three times. I go to the bathroom, get dressed, test my blood sugar, eat breakfast, cover my breakfast (which means take enough insulin to help my body process the food I've eaten), brush my teeth, grab my stuff and, if the weather's good, walk to school with The Lizard. Aside from The Lizard part, I like walking to school because I really like where we live.

Sherwood's a small town in northern New Jersey, really close to the New York border. It's so small we've only got one school for all the kids up to eighth grade, which means you see the same faces every single day for nine years. When I slept over Jonny's last month we compared yearbooks from when we were in kindergarten to last year. It's amazing how little some people have changed since kindergarten. Maureen Haas still wears her hair all pulled over to one side of her head, and our friend Andy Werthy still has that crooked smile that looks like his lower lip is slipping off his face.

About the only thing Sherwood is famous for is the golf course right in the middle of town. Okay, so it's not literally in the middle, but the way people talk about it you'd think it was the Washington Monument or something. Some of the old timers still go on about the summer that they played the U.S. Open at the Sherwood Knolls Golf Club and blah blah blah. Of course, that was back before they discovered electricity, and nothing very exciting has happened here ever since—until I was diagnosed with diabetes a couple of years ago. Now I can't go anywhere in town without someone casually checking up on me.

That's one of the things my mom loves about Sherwood: there's always "a friendly neighbor keeping an eye on things." And by that Mom means "keeping an eye on me." I'm convinced she secretly worries that one day my blood sugar will plummet and I'll collapse in the middle of the street but no one will be around to see it because it'll happen on the same day that the U.S. Open comes back to town and everyone will be at Sherwood Knolls.

The fact of the matter is that it's kind of creepy knowing that people are watching you, especially when they try to act like they're not watching you, and even more especially when you don't want their creepy eyes all over you. Every once in a while, when I'm walking to school or downtown, my neck'll tingle. That's when I know someone's watching.

Anyway, I was running a little behind on Monday on account of my crazy dream. Lizzie whined the whole way about not wanting to be late but then complained that I was walking too fast. We didn't get to school until just before the bell rang, so I wasn't able to talk to Jonny. He just handed me a note that said, "Working on it."

I passed Serena in the hallway between first and second periods. As soon as we made eye contact, I remembered my dream and started to blush. Mortified, I took a sharp left into the first doorway and found myself in the teacher's lounge.

"Can I help you, Caper?"

It was Ms. Fessenden, one of the middle school science teachers.

"Uh, no, thanks, I, uh, just got, um, confused and I, um…" I backed out of there and into the hallway as quickly as I could. I barely made it to second period on time.

The rest of the day was a blur as I kept trying to find time to talk to Jonny alone. It wasn't as easy as I thought it would be. We ended up having to wait until after school.

Jonny and I huddled off to the side of the junior playground while The Lizard played on the monkey bars. She's in kindergarten, and I knew that I only had a few minutes before she got bored and would want to leave—which usually happens when she sees me trying to have a life by talking to someone.

When I saw Jonny, he was looking kind of grim.

"Sorry, Cape," he said. "I came up blank."

I couldn't believe my ears. Jonny Barrish coming up blank? What was the world coming to?

"Nothing?"

"I'm telling you, Caper, this was a toughie," he said. "I went at it at from all angles and couldn't come up with anything worthy of how big a deal this is."

"You're telling me you couldn't come up with one single idea?"

Jonny shrugged and handed me a crumpled piece of paper from his spiral. "It's embarrassing, really. Not my best work. You shouldn't even waste your time reading it."

But of course I did anyway. These were his ideas:

1. Hit your parents with a rolled up newspaper.

2. Put newspaper on the kitchen floor and pee on it.

3. Call your parents by dog names.

4. Make them watch DVDs of old dog movies.

I glanced up at Jonny and saw him wince every time I read one.

"You're right," I said. "Clearly not your best work."

And then, as if sensing that Jonny and I were about to break this problem wide open, Lizzie ran over.

"Caaaaaa-perrrrrrrr! I want to go home now!" She curtsied to Jonny. "Hi, Jonny."

"Hi, Lizzie," Jonny said.

Lizzie tugged at my hand. "Let's go, Caper, I want to go home," she whined. I snatched my hand away.

"Thanks anyway, Jonny," I said. "If I can get to the computer, I'll I.M. you later."

As we walked off the playground, Lizzie said, "What's iyemulater?"

I was trying to think, so I kind of ignored her.

"Iyemulater," she repeated. "You just told Jonny you'd do it to him."

I replayed the conversation in my mind and laughed when I figured out what she meant. "I said I'd I.M. him later."

"Is iye*mimmim*later like iye*mu*later?"

"What are you talking about?" I yelled, my frustration at Jonny's lack of help spilling all over my six year old sister.

"Never mind," Lizzie muttered, her face clouding up.

Now I'd done it. I'd ruined my little sister's perpetually sunny mood. I only had another couple of blocks to cheer her up otherwise I'd be in for the third degree from my mother.

"I.M. is an abbreviation for 'instant message'," I explained. "It's sort of like a combination of talking on the phone and writing an e-mail. So when I said, 'I'll I.M. you later,' I meant that I would send instant messages to Jonny later on today."

"If you could get to the computer," Lizzie added, just to show that had been paying close attention to the original conversation.

I nodded. Lizzie began to skip ahead of me, so I knew the storm clouds had dissolved. Being a big brother can be exhausting.

Our house is second from the corner and looks like it was built right after the U.S. Open was here. It's mostly white with dark red ("merlot" according to my mother) shutters and a dark gray roof. The driveway's on the right side and has a basketball hoop over the garage. It's my job to enter the garage door code because Lizzie can't reach the keypad yet.

We got inside and I dropped my backpack next to the kitchen counter while Lizzie ran to the bathroom. There was a note on the counter from my mom saying she had to run over to Mrs. Walsh's for something and would be back soon. I washed my hands at the kitchen sink and got ready to test my blood, which I have to do like five or six times a day.

Every time I prick my finger I go back to that first night in the hospital when I was diagnosed with Type 1 diabetes, and they kept pricking my fingers every two hours until my blood sugar was under control. When I first got there, my blood sugar was so off-the-charts high that they jabbed a needle into my arm and hooked me up to an I.V. with insulin in it to slowly bring my blood sugar down.

And that first night in the hospital? Well, there's really no word I could use that wouldn't get me sent to my room, so I'll just say it was intensely unpleasant to the millionth degree. With the I.V. in my left arm I wasn't allowed to get out of bed—even to use the bathroom—which meant that I had to pee into a plastic container (about as much fun as it sounds). Also, because of the I.V., I couldn't bend or move my arm, so I had to sleep with my arm laying there next to me. Which brings me back to the fact that I couldn't really sleep anyway because the nurses kept coming in every two hours to prick my fingers with steak knives. Okay, they weren't really steak knives, but they might as well have been. I spent the next few days in the hospital learning all about diabetes and pricking my own fingers and giving myself my own injections of insulin. Again, about as much fun as it sounds.

I remember my first day back at school, everyone was super nice to me. Even Mrs. Melrose, who isn't very nice to anybody except kids on the math team. My mom says that having diabetes made me a minor celebrity, since I was the first kid in school to have diabetes.

One of the few good things about getting diabetes is that all of a sudden I had special privileges, like a permanent all-access hall pass. I go to the nurse's office a few times a day: to check my blood sugar before and after lunch, before gym, and whenever I feel like my sugar's going too low or too high. I keep snacks in the nurse's office for when my blood sugar's low. I also take those stupid standardized tests in a separate room where I can get extra time in case I need to go to the nurse. Some kids still tell me how lucky I am that I can leave class whenever I want and how they wish they could get out of class whenever they wanted. If they really understood that diabetes is something that doesn't go away like a cold or a flu, I don't think they'd want that wish to come true.

So anyway, I tested my blood, and right after the meter announced my blood glucose in big grandma numbers, Lizzie came out of the bathroom and announced, "I want a snack!"

"Good for you," I said, entering the number into my insulin pump with one hand while I grabbed my backpack with the other. When I was halfway up the stairs, I heard Lizzie's voice.

"Ca-perrrrr!"

I stopped and rolled my eyes.

"What?" I replied, my voice flat and irritated.

"Can you please pour me some lemonade?" she asked.

"NO!" I wanted to shout back. "Get your own lemonade!" But I didn't, because I knew if I did I'd be dead meat. I also knew that Lizzie's history with pouring things wasn't so good, and unless I wanted to spend the rest of the afternoon mopping up after her, I'd better do it myself. So I dropped my backpack on the steps and trudged back downstairs.

"What was your number?" she asked.

"None of your business," I snapped, grabbing the pitcher of sugar-free lemonade from the fridge.

"Was it a hundred twenty eight?" she asked.

"No," I said.

"A million-eleventy-seven?"

"No!"

"Six?"

"NO!"

"Can I test my blood too?" she asked, gazing at my testing kit.

I finished pouring the lemonade, put it back in the fridge, grabbed my kit and stormed out of the kitchen before I said or did something to Lizzie I would regret.

"You forgot to write your number on the chart!" were the last words of Lizzie's I heard as I went into my room and slammed the door. I dropped my backpack and threw myself down on my bed. I could barely stand it when my mother nagged me about my diabetes, but when The Lizard started in...well, that was too much. I screamed into my pillow a couple of times and kicked the bean bag chair by the foot of my bed. Feeling a little better, I took a deep breath and surveyed my room.

It's not as big as Jonny's new room but it's all right. It's got all your basic furniture: bed, dresser, desk, some shelves on the wall for books and stuff. There's also a closet and my dad's old computer on a portable computer cart. When I was ten my parents let me choose a new paint color, so my room is all dark blue (except for one white wall because my mother insisted on a contrast color to keep the room from looking like "a cave"). I've been begging my parents for a new computer of my own since the one I currently use is about a hundred years old. I was hoping to get one as sort of a "we're sorry you got diabetes" present, but that didn't happen. Though they won't admit it, I think my parents are afraid that I'd use it to gamble away all our money in poker rooms.

As I lay on my bed, I thought about Jonny's list and then remembered my dream when I was in the closet and suddenly something clicked inside, like a switch. In a single flash, I had it! The idea was brilliant in its simplicity, and I was getting pumped just thinking about the possibilities. My parents named me after a dog. So why not become the dog they always wished they had for a son?

TUESDAY

Tuesday morning my mother announced that Lizzie was going home with Melanie Ewing for a play date.

"And I'm going to be help set up the plant sale," she added. "But just until four. Why don't you come and help?"

There was nothing my mother wouldn't do to keep me from being alone…just in case, you know? Even if something happened to me yesterday after school, I at least had Lizzie around to call for help.

The last thing I wanted to do was hang out with my mother at school when I could use those same fifty-two minutes to start working on my plan. Mom must've seen me frown.

"Or I can call Jonny's mother and tell her you'll walk home with Jonny."

"Great idea!" I said.

"I see," Mom said, her smile melting away.

"No, I mean, I'd love to hang out with you and the plants, Mom…"

"That's all right, Caper," she said, reaching for the phone.

Wonderful. Only my mother could make me feel guilty about not wanting to spend time with her so I could work on my plan to get even with her. But the feeling lingered only as long as I was in the house. Once The Lizard and I left, my brain shifted gears to me and Jonny walking downtown so I could start working on my plan. I couldn't wait to get to school to find Jonny and begin strategizing.

Our school, Sherwood Consolidated School, goes from kindergarten to eighth grade, but they do their best to keep us separated. For instance, in the morning, the little kids gather by their playground on one end of the building. The second and third graders use the front entrance. And fourth through eighth graders use the two entrances on the far side of the building. The fourth and fifth graders use the lower door, and the middle school uses the upper door.

There's enough space on the blacktop and grass for everyone to spread out, so each of the grades has its own unofficial area. The seventh graders occupy the middle area of the blacktop, sort of spilling over a bit onto the grass. And the eighth graders—who consider themselves way too cool for anyone else in the school—gather in small groups about as far as you can go from the upper door and still hear the morning bell. So that leaves us sixth graders hovering around the upper door.

That morning as I cut through the crowd, I spied Jonny talking to Andy Werthy (the kid with the crooked smile, remember?) and Walker Munroe. These are the guys I hang out with the most. And also Skip Cristis, who was totally in his hackey-sack zone and oblivious to everything else. In fact, that was sort of Skip's approach to a lot of things. He was always there but not always there, if you know what I mean. It was funny seeing him with a hackey-sack of all things, because Skip's one of those kids who can't seem to walk down the street without something happening to him.

From the moment he and his twin sister Mary got to the school in first grade, he has broken both arms and one leg (not at the same time, of course), had chicken pox, and dropped his lunch on the floor in the cafeteria more times than I can remember. The thing is, he's a really nice guy who usually has a smile on his face when he isn't recovering from dental surgery.

Jonny once asked me that if I could trade my diabetes for everything that happens to Skip Cristis, would I do it. I thought about it, but I'm not so sure I would, because at least with my diabetes, I sort of know what I'm dealing with. I'm not so sure I could say that if I were Skip Cristis.

Anyway, that Tuesday morning I walked up to the guys and heard them arguing about video games.

"...and there's no way they're releasing the video game before the movie comes out!" Walker said.

"They do it all the time!" Andy shouted back. "They did it with 'Rocket Skulls' and 'Deathscapades'!"

If there's one thing I'm not into, it's video games. They give me headaches. I pulled Jonny aside and told him we needed to figure out a way to get his mom to let us walk home by ourselves (through town, of course).

"Man! I'd give anything to go with you, Caper," he said. "But it's Guitar Lesson Tuesday. Plus there's my brother."

I had totally forgotten about Jonny's guitar lessons, and his younger brother for that matter.

"Then I need you to help me come up with an excuse for when I don't come home with you and Eric," I said. "You know your mom, so make it a good one."

The bell rang and we headed inside. Now if I could only get those six hours of school out of the way, I could focus on the really important things...like revenge!

During lunch, Jonny showed me the list of excuses he had come up with:

1. *Didn't feel well (diabetes) and went home early.*

2. *Lizzie's playdate got cancelled so you took her home.*

3. *Date with Serena Kingsley.*

4. *Stayed to help with the plant sale.*

I read through the list and ticked off my problems with each of the excuses.

1. Can't mess around with my diabetes because then Jonny's mom would call my mom to find out how I was feeling.

2. Too risky, especially if Lizzie got wind of it, she'd blow the whole thing.

3. My response? I punched Jonny in the arm.

4. Had possibilities.

By the time the bell finally rang at 3:05 PM, I had it all figured out. I told Jonny to go with Number 4. Then I went to the PTA room, a tiny classroom in the old wing of the building where the moms did all of their planning and stuff, to find my mother.

"Hey, mom," I said. "Hey, Mrs. Trammel."

"How are you, Caper?" asked Mrs. Trammel.

"Fine, thanks."

"How was your day, sweetie?" Mom asked.

"Good," I said. "Lots of homework though. Anyway, here I am."

"Yes, you are," Mom said. "Is Jonny with you?"

"No, he went home with Eric," I said.

Mom look puzzled. "You were supposed to go home with him and Eric, too, remember? I told you this morning."

"I know," I nodded. "But then I got second thoughts about helping so I told him I'd just stay, but that was at lunch before I knew how much homework I had."

That really threw Mom. "I'm not sure I understand, Caper. Are you saying you want to stay and help?"

"I did, but then I got all this homework."

"So…"

If there was going to be a moment when I'd crack, this was it. I was about to lie to my mother, something I'd never done before. Well, something I'd never done with so much planning anyway. All I had to do was remember that the reason I was lying was because they lied to me first, and all my hesitations melted away.

"If it's all right, I'd rather go straight home so I can start on my homework."

"How much homework do you have?"

I shrugged. "Um, a couple pages of math. A language arts sheet. No, two language arts sheets. A science something or other, and study for the math test on Thursday. Plus my Hebrew school stuff."

I could tell my mom was trying to calculate how much work that actually was, but before she could finish, I gave her the full-court press. I took my blood testing kit out of my backpack and checked my blood.

"One-twelve, nothing active, no correction," I reported. I must admit, it was a pretty good number, not too high, not too low, right in the middle of the target zone of 80-120. It must have been the magic number, because my mother slowly nodded her head.

"Well, I'm not thrilled with you being home alone, Caper," she said. "Once you got all this homework you should have stuck to the original plan. But I guess it's too late now." She paused and pursed her lips. The anticipation was killing me. "But it's only till four and your number's really good. So walk straight home and call me. And if you have a snack, remember to test again and put the number in your pump with the carbs. And come to think of it, did you put this number in your pump?"

"Already done!"

I was genuinely happy that she was letting me go. It was the first time in a long time she was letting me go anywhere by myself. And I knew it was because she trusted me, so I admit I did feel a little guilty. But the feeling passed as soon as I stepped outside and turned right onto Sherwood Avenue. Three blocks later I turned left onto Main Street and strolled into beautiful "downtown" Sherwood.

"Downtown" Sherwood is exactly one block long and consists of a pizza place, a dry cleaners, two hair places (I still don't get that), a hardware store, post office, two doctors, four lawyers, a 24-hour deli that's open only about fifteen hours on a good day, and the General Store, which was my destination.

The real name of the place is Sherwood Gift & Beauty, but everyone calls it the General Store because they still have part of the original sign up from when it was called the General Store back when that stupid golf tournament was here. And for an old-fashioned sounding place, the General Store has a pretty cool assortment of things. It's a combination drug store-card store-gift shop-candy store-newsstand-and notary public.

I blew into the General Store and made a bee line for one particular rack of merchandise sandwiched between the greeting cards and pukey-smelling bath soaps and candles. I grabbed the exact item I wanted and turned to go pay, but then turned back. Why not go all the way? I counted how much money I had in my pocket and did some quick math. I took two other items and held them low against my leg so as not to draw anyone's attention to them. The last thing I needed was a set of "neighborly eyes" sneaking a peek at what I was doing. I gave the stuff to Mrs. Sweeney behind the counter, who rang it up and asked, "Cash or house charge, hun?"

She asked me a couple of times, but I didn't hear her because my head was filling up with helium. Not literally, of course, but that's what it felt like. I instantly recognized one of the signs of my blood sugar starting to drop. Something on my face must have alarmed the old lady cashier, because the next thing I knew Barbara the pharmacist was standing next to me.

"You feeling all right, Caper?" she asked.

I nodded. Something about her voice brought things back into focus.

"Need some glucose tablets or anything?" she said.

I shook my head and told her I had a juice box in my backpack but had to test my blood first. I reached behind and unzipped the side compartment just enough to squeeze my hand in. While I grappled around for my testing kit, Mrs. Sweeney put the things on the counter into a white "Sherwood Gift and Beauty" bag.

"I'll just put these on your parents' account," she said.

"No!" I shouted, twisting my arm out of the backpack so suddenly that I pulled a muscle in my shoulder. "DANG IT!"

Barbara and Mrs. Sweeney looked at me. So did Mrs. Rutledge, little Pippa Rutledge, and everyone else in the General Store. I lowered my head mumbled an apology.

"I'd like to pay cash, if it's all right," I said. "They're sort of a..."

"Present?" Mrs. Sweeney asked with a smile.

"More like a surprise," I replied.

I pulled the money from my pocket and dropped it on the counter. I knew I was supposed to test my blood so I could see how low I was going, but I didn't have time—I needed to get home before my mother. After I stuffed my purchases inside, I rooted around the bottom of the backpack and found my kit and a juice box. I popped the straw in and sucked down the juice in about two seconds.

"You going to check your blood sugar?" Barbara asked. It was amazing how everyone in the world could say that to me without a hint of nagging—everyone except my parents, of course. I nodded.

"Yeah, I'll do it on the bench outside," I said. I zipped up my bag, threw it over my shoulder, and took off out the back door. I had to get home, so I had no intention of sitting on the bench outside. I plodded along in slow motion until I could feel the sugar from the juice kicking in. Now that Step One of the plan was complete, I was ready for Step Two—whatever that was.

When I got home, I wanted to go directly upstairs, but a nagging voice at the back of my head told me to check my blood. So I did and found that it was seventy-nine. It must have been pretty low back at the General Store if it only got back up to seventy-nine from one-twelve. That's one of the things about having diabetes. Since my pancreas can't make insulin and regulate my blood sugar like everyone else, I get these occasional lows (and highs) where things go wacky.

Anyway, I was feeling better, so I went up to my room and closed the door. I dumped the bag out on my bed and took stock of my inventory. I threaded the blue nylon dog leash with white paw prints through the loops of my jeans. I draped the green, blue, and red tie-dye bandana over my shoulders and tied it in front. I fastened the black leather dog collar with rows of tiny silver spikes snugly around my neck. I looked in the mirror and smiled. Facing me was Caper Spiegelman in all his canine glory.

"They wanted a dog for a son?" I announced defiantly. "They've got one!"

It was at this point that the phone rang and I practically shot through the roof. It took me a second to come back to earth, and when I did, a feeling of dread filled me up inside. I forgot to call Mom.

Oh, God, I thought. What if she ran into Mrs. Rutledge? Or Mrs. Sweeney? They'd tell her I was in the General Store! I couldn't even bear to think what was going to happen next. She'd find out about my little episode *and* all the stuff I bought. The only thing I was certain of was that I only had one more ring before the answering machine picked up. I charged downstairs to the kitchen and grabbed the handset.

"Yello!" I said as cheerfully as I could.

"Hello, Mr. Happiness," my mother said. "You forget something?"

"Yeah, I am so sorry, Mom," I said. "I got home and totally forgot. I was thinking about the math test and, well, I'm really, really sorry."

My mother paused as if she were filtering my words through the Lie-O-Meter. "So did you eat anything or test again?" Her words were clipped, and there was no warmth in her voice.

"Seventy-nine," I answered.

"Did you put it on the chart?" she asked. I told her I had...as I penciled it in.

"Good," she continued. "Anyway, we're on our way home."

"We?"

"Lizzie and I," Mom said.

"But I thought The Lizard was at Melanie's," I said, sensing the panic that began creeping into my voice.

"She was, but Melanie's mother called me because Melanie threw up. That pretty much put an end to her playdate. Besides, I'm pulling into the driveway now."

As the words left her mouth, I heard the garage door open.

"See ya," I said, hanging up.

The van door slammed shut and Lizzie's footsteps echoed in the garage. I shook my head in frustration and felt something scratching my neck. The dog collar! I looked down and realized I was still wearing the leash and bandana too! The knob on the door to the garage rattled.

"Open up, Caper!" Lizzie shouted through the door.

I could not let them see me. I tore off the bandana and yanked at the leash, snapping two belt loops as the nylon strip snaked its way around my waist.

"Caper, you maniac!" Lizzie screamed. "Unlock the door!"

"Honestly, Lizzie," my mother said, "I've got the key right here."

I turned round and round hoping to find a magic door in the kitchen that I could disappear through. But since one wasn't handy, I ducked into the downstairs bathroom and slammed the door just as Lizzie bounded into the kitchen.

"You wouldn't believe all that throw-up!" Lizzie yelled with a little too much excitement in her voice. "We were playing dolls and Melanie looked up and her face had a funny look on it and her nose scrunched up and then her cheeks puffed up and she turned her head and threw up right onto the doll house! It was tan and chunky and I saw some of the chocolate chips from the cookies—"

"That's enough, Lizzie!" Mom said. "I told you in the car I didn't want to hear about it! Caper?"

"I'm in here," I yelled through the door. In the privacy of the bathroom, I was able to focus on unfastening the collar without scraping the bejeebies out of my neck.

"Are you all right?" Mom asked.

"Are you throwing up?" Lizzie called.

"Can't a guy use the bathroom?" I shot back.

I heard my mother walk towards the bathroom and pause just outside the door.

"Were you in there when we were just on the phone?" she asked. "Wait, I don't think I want to know the answer to that." She walked back through the kitchen. "I have to go deliver a couple of plants. I'll be right back. Please don't torment your sister."

I let out my breath as I heard the door close again. I looked in the mirror and smiled.

"The call was close," I whispered. I rolled up the leash, collar and bandana in a towel and stepped into the hallway. Everything was quiet. Too quiet. The Lizard was skulking around somewhere. But I thought that if I moved quickly enough, I could make it back upstairs before she had a chance to pull whatever it was that she planned to pull.

I took big, stealthy strides through the kitchen, dining room and up the stairs. At the top, I smiled again, knowing I had made it. Just as I crossed to my room, I heard it:

"GOTCHA!"

Lizzie jumped out from behind my door and sent my heart up into my throat. I jumped back, dropped the towel and threw myself against the wall for support. The metal clasp of the

31

leash dangled out one side of the towel roll and hit the hardwood floor with a THUNK.

Lizzie and I looked down at the towel, and then at each other.

"What's in the towel?" she asked.

"Nothing," I said.

This was what you would call a stand-off. Lizzie and I stared at each other, neither one moving. I had to be very careful. One false move and it'd all be over. But while I was thinking of what to do, Lizzie sprang into action. You see, Lizzie is fast. Very fast. And her hands were on the towel before I could bend halfway down. This was a delicate situation, one that required quick and decisive action. There was no way I could let Lizzie see what was rolled up inside the towel. She'd blab it to my parents and ruin the whole thing and then I'd never get my sweet revenge. No, I couldn't let her end up with that towel. But I was at a complete loss. And I was desperate. So I did the only thing I could think.

"Okay, Lizzie, you win, you can—whoa," I said, slapping my hand out against the wall to keep me from falling over. The response was instantaneous.

"What is it?" Lizzie asked. "Are you okay? Should I call Mom?"

I raised my other hand to my forehead.

"No...no...I'm fine," I said, squeezing out the words like the last drops of ketchup. "It's just I...I..."

"What? Is it your diabetes numbers?" Lizzie said, stepping closer.

"GOTCHA!" I whispered.

I yanked the towel from Lizzie's hands, shot into my room, and slammed the door.

"Caper, you maniac! That's not funny! You're like the boy who cried wolf! Next time you're dying from diabetes, don't come crying to me!" She ran into her room and slammed the door.

I admit it wasn't one of the nicer things I've ever done to The Lizard. I mean, even though she's a pain, she's a pretty good sister sometimes with all the diabetes stuff. But I couldn't risk blowing everything now. I needed to maintain complete secrecy. And with Lizzie tucked away in her room, I had a few minutes of peace and quiet to regroup and figure out what I was going to do next.

I was on pins and needles all Tuesday night, making it hard to concentrate on my actual homework that really didn't take all that long to do. I was waiting for my mom or dad to come into my room and read me the riot act about using my diabetes to trick The Lizard like that. Every footstep on the stairs sent my heart into overdrive. And dinner was unbearable. Maybe all the guilt and worrying was my punishment. All I know is that when my mom came up to have me test before bed, I was on the verge of confessing. Turns out I didn't have to, because Lizzie apparently hadn't said anything to my parents.

Little sisters. Go figure.

WEDNESDAY

The next morning, there were still no signs that my parents knew anything, so I finally let myself relax. I got to school before Jonny and went over to Andy and Walker. Skip was also there, still working on his hackey-sacking.

"Caper, c'mere!" Andy said. I leaned in with Andy and Walker. Andy whispered, "Mary's having a party."

"Cool," I said. "When is it?"

"I'm not sure," Andy said.

"Who's invited?" I asked.

"Dunno," Walker shrugged.

That's when Jonny came over.

"What's going on?" he asked.

"Sherlock Holmes and Watson here heard that Mary's having a party but have no idea when it is or who's invited."

Jonny looked at Andy and Walker. "Didja think of asking, oh, I don't know, say, Mary's twin brother?"

Andy and Walker looked at each other and then at Skip. They waved him over.

"Hey, Skip, what's up with Mary's party?" Andy asked.

Skip's eyes lit up. "Mary's having a party?"

Jonny and I laughed and left Andy and Walker alone with Skip. I pulled Jonny aside and told him about the stuff I had bought.

"Sweet," Jonny nodded. "So what's your next step?"

"I was hoping you'd have some ideas," I said.

Jonny nodded some more. "I'm on it. Give me till after school."

The bell rang and we all tramped inside to begin another boring and useless day at Sherwood Consolidated School.

Up to fourth grade, we stayed in our classrooms for everything. In fifth, we switched classes for either math, science or social studies, depending on your teacher's specialty. And once we got to sixth, we started changing classes every period. This year, my favorite class is social studies, and it's not because Mrs. Stuyvesant gives us the least amount of homework. It's because I get to sit at a table with Serena Kingsley.

I've known Serena since kindergarten and have gotten to know her in the way you get to know anyone you've been around your entire life without actually living with them. We say "hi" and are always friendly and have some of the same friends and see each other at various parties and things during the year, but aside from a random playdate in kindergarten, we never really hung out together.

Then just before school started, I caught a glimpse of her at the General Store buying school supplies. She turned and waved at me, and I could swear that a little spark shot off from her fingertips and zapped me. Now I have a hard time looking at her without feeling that same zappiness.

Anyway, during lunch, I recapped the events of Tuesday afternoon for Jonny and then asked him the big question: When should I make my move?

Jonny didn't miss a beat. "That's easy," he said, taking a bite of his tuna fish sandwich. "At dinner with your aunt on Saturday."

I was stunned.

"I'm having dinner with my aunt on Saturday?" I asked. "How do you know?"

Jonny leaned in. "I never told you this, but I can see the future in my eye. By the way, when you're twenty-eight, don't get on that flight to Jamaica." He took another bite.

"What? Really?"

"You're such a moe-head!" Jonny said. "Of course I'm not psychic. I heard them talking about it when your mom called about switching carpool dates. Just show up during the meal with your dog stuff on and confront your parents."

"You mean I should wear that stuff out in public?" I gasped. "Are you crazy?"

"Think about it, Cape," Jonny said. "It's really the perfect set up. First of all, your parents won't make a scene in a public place. Second, they'll be more embarrassed than you could ever be. And third, you'll have your aunt there for back up."

I began playing out the scene in my mind. I pictured us all in a restaurant with me walking over dressed as a dog. Before I can even say anything, my mother begins to cry and begs my forgiveness. Even my father gets choked up and apologizes. Aunt Connie's crying eye kicks into gear, and Lizzie…well, Lizzie sits there eating chocolate pudding.

"Hmmm…not bad, maestro." I gave Jonny a pat on the back. We scarfed down the rest of our lunch just as the bell was ringing. Jonny went straight to class and I headed for the nurse's office.

"Feeling lucky today, Caper?" Nurse Bevilaqua asked. Once, her ninety-five-year-old mother played the lottery with my blood glucose numbers for the day and won fifty dollars. Ever since then, the nurse asks if I'm feeling lucky. I gave her my carb count from lunch, watched her record it on my chart, and then entered the number into my insulin pump.

If you've never seen an insulin pump, it's a mini-computer about the size of a deck of cards that figures out how much insulin I need based on a whole bunch of numbers and formulas. I wear it clipped to my belt or pants, and it's got a thin little tube that connects to another little tube that goes under my skin. Basically, I tell it how many carbohydrates I've eaten and it knows how much insulin to give me to get the glucose from those carbs into my cells for energy. I don't want to bore you with all the crazy details. All I'll say is that the pump makes it so I don't have to take shots all day long, which is fine by me.

The rest of the day was relatively normal. I spent most of it dividing my time between paying attention and planning out the details of my grand entrance on Saturday night. When it was time to leave, I stopped by my locker.

"Caper?"

I froze. Mary Christis's voice always made my spine tingle. I slowly turned around and saw her standing there beside Serena. Serena smiled, but Mary did all the talking.

"Are you doing anything next Saturday night? Not this Saturday night, but next Saturday night. For some reason, people have a hard time with that. Well?"

"Uh, no," I shrugged. "Why?"

"We're having a party at my house and you're invited. Are you coming?"

Between Mary's laser-like gaze and Serena's smile, all I could do was shrug and say something like "Isinkso."

"I'll e-mail you the details." With that, Mary and Serena left.

I stood there a second while my brain re-booted itself. Still in a bit of a daze, I walked outside and caught sight of Skip practicing with his hackey sack. I turned and took no more than three steps when I heard Skip fall to the ground with a dull THUD.

"I'm okay!" he called out to no one in particular.

I'm telling you, being diabetic has nothing on being Skip Cristis.

After dinner that night, I checked my e-mail. Andy had forwarded some stupid jokes, and Walker sent me something about his fantasy baseball team. Jonny and I I.M.ed about my "big" dinner on Saturday and Mary's party next week. There was a message from our math teacher about an extra-credit worksheet we could download, and there was something from Aunt Connie. I saved her e-mail for last.

Hey, Caper. Looking forward to dinner Saturday. Got a surprise for you. Luv, AC

Surprise? For me? I wondered what she meant. But I didn't want to sound like a six year old getting all excited about a surprise, so I tried to play it cool when I wrote back:

aunt connie. i've got one too. see you saturday.

So there it was. I had put it in writing so there was no turning back. True, I didn't tell her what the surprise was, so if I changed my mind and chickened out she'd never know. But then I realized that if I did change my mind and chicken out, I wouldn't have a surprise so then I'd need to have some kind of back-up surprise ready just in case.

Another perfect example of my mind getting ahead of my brain, you know?

THURSDAY

Thursday morning I arrived at school and I immediately began to feel strange. It was the same feeling I had my first day back after being diagnosed with diabetes. Back then, I felt people looking at me. I felt their eyes trying to look inside my body to see what was wrong with me. I felt their stares crawling over my skin to see what diabetes looks like. But there weren't any rashes, scars, bald patches, or even band-aids to satisfy their curiosity. I was my same old regular self, which probably made things even weirder. Kids at school are used to seeing crutches and casts and even the occasional wheelchair, but when someone's sick and has nothing to show for it, that person stands out even more.

Anyway, that's what I felt like on Thursday morning. And I didn't like it. I didn't see Jonny, so I caught up to Andy and Walker.

"What's going on?" I asked.

Andy and Walker looked at me funny. Walker has this nervous laugh that drives me crazy, and this morning it was in full force.

"Don't sweat it, Caper," he said. "I mean no one really cares, you know?"

"About what?" I asked, my "spider sense" telling me something was definitely up.

Andy and Walker shot a glance at the lower door. There was hand-drawn poster taped to it. As I got closer, my throat tightened and I felt my heart begin to pound. Blood rushed to my head and my cheeks burned fiercely as I read the bold red block letters scrawled over a very crude drawing of a dog dressed in jeans and a green jacket with a red flowing cape. The big letters said, "The Adventures of Dog-Boy!" And there, in tiny letters beneath the drawing of the dog, it said, *By day, he's mild-mannered student Caper Spiegeldog. But when he's had too much sugar he becomes the amazing Dog-Boy!*

I was utterly speechless, and not in a brain-freeze kind of way, but in an overwhelmingly angry and hurt and embarrassed kind of way. I couldn't even begin to wrap my brain around who could have done this.

"Caper!"

I turned around and there was Jonny. The only person in the world I told. The only other person in the world who knew. Jonny. My best friend.

"Thanks for nothing!" I spat.

Fortunately, the bell rang so I didn't have to do or say anything else. To be honest, I don't know what I would have done, so it's just as well. On my way in, I ripped the poster down and tore it into as many pieces as I could. I gave myself a good paper-cut in the process, but I didn't care. As I tore up the poster I felt like I was tearing up my friendship with Jonny.

It's hard to avoid your best friend, but I did my best. I tried to lose myself in my class work, but that was impossible. I pretty much kept to myself at lunch. Andy made a token attempt to cheer me up, but even his usual goofiness didn't work. Even Serena must have felt like something was wrong, because during all of lunch, she kept glancing over at me. It was supremely weird. She'd look up and make eye contact, hold it just long enough to make me tingle, and then dive right back into her conversation. Once I even thought I saw her start to get up in my direction. Did she want to tell me something? My head was such a mess, I had no idea what was going on. Finally, the lunch aides herded us out of the cafeteria and that was that.

Somehow, I made it through my math test and the rest of the day, but after school wasn't any better. First, I had to walk Lizzie home from school, and she chattered the whole way about the class's pet iguana and jello and I don't know what else. Sometimes I really don't know where she came from.

When I got home, I had just enough time to test my blood, grab a snack, and then jump into the car for Hebrew School. It was my mom's turn to drive, which means I got to sit up front, which was fine by me since I was still mad at Jonny. When Jonny and Eric got in, Jonny said hi to my mom and to me. I sort of grunted in response. We picked up Shari Grubarsky, who's also in my grade and belongs to my temple, and she and my mother chatted the whole way to temple. Hebrew school was an absolute bore. I've been in Hebrew school since third grade, and the best thing about it was having Jonny there— until today, that is.

By the time we got home it was dinner time. My mood really hadn't gotten any better, but at least I felt safe from the outside world—a feeling that wasn't going to last very long. You see, once dinner started and everyone talked about their day, my father took a bite of Italian bread and asked,

"Now, Caper, what's this I hear about you almost collapsing in the General Store the other day?"

My father has excellent timing. Not in the "telling a joke" sense, but in the "causing maximum discomfort" sense. Which is probably why he waited for me to take a sip of water before asking the question. As soon as the words left his mouth, my throat closed up tight as a drum so all I could do was spit it back out onto my plate. Lizzie burst into laughter and almost fell off her chair.

I started coughing, and my mother reached over and tried patting me between the shoulder blades, but I waved her off. My father sat there and stared at me. He had asked a question and was now waiting for a response. I knew that the longer it took, the more it would look like I was making something up. But I needed more time, so I padded my little fit with some additional coughs and throat clearings.

You know, the biggest problem with all those "neighborly eyes" watching out for you is that they're always attached to neighborly mouths. I thought back to who was also at the General Store on Tuesday. First I thought it was Pippa Rutledge, that pipsqueak. Then I remembered she's afraid of my father. Plus, I couldn't really picture a scenario where my father would be having a conversation with a six year old who wasn't my sister. The more I thought about that, in fact, the funnier it seemed. I must have started smiling, because my mother said,

"This isn't a laughing matter, Caper."

The cartoon bubble in my mind burst, and I saw the disappointment on my mother's face. My cheeks burned and my mind locked up in what was becoming an exceedingly annoying and badly-timed habit. I heard a little voice in the back of my brain shouting, over and over, "Why didn't you plan an excuse? Why aren't you prepared?"

Why aren't you prepared? Be prepared. Always have a plan.

These were the things that my mother tried to drill into my head when I was first diagnosed. Until there was a cure, she said, we couldn't beat the diabetes, but we could control it. And the best way to control it is to always be prepared. "Always have your testing kit with you. Always have a snack in case of low blood sugar. Always have a water bottle in case of high blood sugar." You know, you hear something enough times over and over, it's like you can't hear it anymore. And even though those words were burned into my brain and have really served me well when it comes to my diabetes, I never seemed to be able to make them work for anything else in my life. And now I was going to pay. Dearly.

"Caper, you told your mother you were walking straight home. But did you go straight home?"

"I never said I was going to go *straight* home," I mumbled. Technically, I knew I was right. But my dad's a lawyer, and he wasn't buying what I was selling.

"Caper, the real problem for me is that you put yourself in danger by not coming straight home," he said. "Something could have happened to you if your blood sugar got too low. Did you even test at the General Store to see what your number was?"

I shook my head and apologized. I felt my throat tighten and my cheeks get hot. Please, no tears, I pleaded to myself. And then, after what felt like an eternity, my father shoveled another forkful of lasagna into his mouth.

"What were you doing at the General Store after school anyway?"

I smiled slightly and said, "I, uh, needed to pick some things up."

"What kind of things?" Mom asked.

"I needed to pick something up for a friend."

"A friend," Mom echoed. "Is it Jonny's birthday or something?"

Jonny? Why was she talking about that traitor? She must have seen the surprise and anger in my face.

"And what's going on with you two?" she asked. "You were very cold to him in the car today."

"Nothing," I said, sounding so unconvincing that even Lizzie picked up on it.

"They had a fight and I know why," she announced. I froze, afraid of what was going to come tumbling out of her mouth. "They fought about a girl."

My dad's eyebrows shot up and he looked at me. "A girl?"

"Yup," Lizzie said. "Boys are always fighting over girls. Pippa Rutledge told me."

Well, that ended that conversation. Anything that Lizzie says that begins or ends with "Pippa Rutledge told me" is automatically thrown into the garbage can because little Pippa is known for simply making things up...though she is very convincing about it. We all went back to eating, but my mother didn't want to let me off the hook, at least not yet.

"If it wasn't for Jonny, who were you getting something for?"

Lizzie announced, "I can touch my eyeball!" Before anyone could protest, she reached up with her right index finger, pulled down the skin beneath her right eye, looked up to the ceiling, and touched the white part of her eyeball with her middle finger. "See?"

"Please, Lizzie, eyeball-touching is not appropriate for the dinner table," Dad said. Then he looked at my mother and added, "Now there's a sentence I never thought I'd have to say out loud."

Despite Lizzie's interruption, Mom would simply not let it go. She looked at me with questioning eyes, and that's when I got an idea. I tilted my head in Lizzie's direction and whispered, "It's sort of a surprise. For someone."

My mom caught on right away that I was talking about Lizzie, but not my dad.

"What? Who's the surprise for?" he asked, taking another bite of bread.

At this point, Mom leaped to my rescue, and I knew I was home free.

"Someone of the female persuasion," she said. She tried to guide my father's gaze over to Lizzie, but he was oblivious.

"A girlfriend?" my dad asked.

Lizzie's head popped up like a Jack-in-the-box.

"Caper has a girlfriend?" she gasped. "I knew it! It's Maureen Haas, isn't it! No, Shari Bubarkey! Wait, is it Snemena Smithkin?"

Mom, Dad and I looked at Lizzie.

"Who?" I asked.

"Sereeninin Kingking," she said.

"You mean Serena Kingsley?" I said.

"Yeah, her!" Lizzie answered.

My face caught fire because of course I couldn't admit that I liked her in front of my parents and certainly not The Lizard so I had to make it clear that just the opposite was true. But somehow saying something like "I'd rather pluck my eyes out with a fork than have Serena Kingsley as a girlfriend!" wouldn't work either because I'd blush twice as hard and turn as red as our merlot-colored shutters. So I decided the best thing to do was to laugh along with everyone else at Lizzie's little mispronunciation. The laughing helped, because I began to feel a little bit better. And it was just as well, because little did I know that Friday was going to be the day I lost the rest of my friends.

FRIDAY

So Friday morning I woke up so wrapped up in everything going on that I guess I ate breakfast without thinking. And that's when my mother started in on me.

"Caper! Did you test?" she asked, her voice brimming with panic.

I had forgotten to test my blood. I put my spoon down and shook my head.

"Honestly, Caper, I can't stay on top of you every minute," Mom said. "You have to take some responsibility for your diabetes management."

About a million words swarmed around me head. Things like "Are you kidding me? This is the first time I've forgotten to test in like three months!" and "Lay off, lady!" and "Oh, no! I forgot to test! The world's coming to an end!" But I knew that anything remotely sarcastic would only make things worse, and my goal was get out of the house as quickly as possible. So

I decided to go with "Sorry," and leave it at that. I tested my blood, put the number in my pump along with my breakfast carb numbers, scooped up my books, and went straight to the door.

"What about me?" Lizzie called, still eating her cereal.

"I'll drive you, dear," Mom said, probably sensing that it was best to let me be by myself that morning. "If I can count on your brother to walk to school without any detours."

Zing! Mom finally got her payback.

I think there was a full minute or two on my walk to school when I was thinking of something pleasant, because I remember feeling my face relax. That was the feeling I missed, that carefree feeling that I used take for granted, when life was simple and I wasn't diabetic and still had a best friend.

When I got to school, I saw Andy, Walker, and Jonny talking. Great. I really wanted to talk to Andy and Walker, but I couldn't do that with Jonny there. I saw Skip playing a hand-held video game but he was having trouble because his left wrist was in some kind of brace. And I saw Serena and Mary chatting with their friends, and for the life of me I couldn't remember what Serena and I talked about at lunch the day before.

It was just as well. I resigned myself to laying low that morning and was making my way over to the door when I heard it. The noise started off sort of distant, like it came from the far end of the blacktop. At first, I wasn't even sure I had heard it all, but then I heard it again. There was no mistaking it now. One of the eighth graders thought it would be hilarious to bark as I passed by. The next thing I knew, kids were barking all over the place. I felt my face burn up while someone pushed me from behind. One of my biggest fears had always been getting beaten up in the school year. It had never happened to me, but I was sure that the shove I felt was the beginning of the end...my end.

I felt the push again and spun around, only to see Andy, Walker and Jonny pushing me into the school building. That was a big deal, because you weren't supposed to go inside the building until the bell rang. Once inside the hallway, I couldn't hear the barking anymore, but I could see through the glass that a bunch of the eighth graders were laughing.

"You okay, Cape?" Walker asked.

"Say the word, and I'll kick their butts," Andy offered. We all laughed because we knew that the eighth graders would have Andy for lunch.

"Thanks," I said, avoiding eye contact. "This really sucks, you know?"

I caught Jonny glaring at Andy and Walker. They looked at him and then at each other. Jonny pulled away from us and went back outside.

"Caper..." Walker began.

"Uh, me and Walker have something to tell you," Andy continued.

The two of them shifted around a bit like all of a sudden their bodies didn't fit anymore.

"You know how someone put that poster up yesterday?" Walker asked.

What a stupid question! Of course I knew! So I didn't answer, I just stared at them.

"Well...Jonny didn't have anything to do with it," Walker said.

"I get it. Jonny told you to tell me that so I wouldn't be mad at him anymore," I said, finally seeing the full depths of my former best-friend's desperation. "Nice. Real nice."

Andy shook his head. "No, Caper, Jonny didn't tell anyone anything." He looked at Walker again, and they both looked down. "We...sort of did."

"WHAT?!" I couldn't believe my ears. "You?! No way! Impossible! I never told you, so how could you have told anyone else?"

And this is where Andy and Walker's faces changed a little. They went from being really sorry looking to a little...well, I don't know what the word is, but they started looking like they were proud of something.

"We, uh, have sort of a hobby that we never told you about," Andy said. Walker spit out a little laugh. He looked at me and went serious again. I'm guessing my expression wasn't the most friendly.

"Basically, we collect people's computer passwords and read their e-mails," Andy said. I didn't say anything, so I guess Walker took that as a sign that I wanted to hear more.

"We started doing it last year, but weren't very good at it," he explained. "Then over the summer we worked out a system that we started using in September. One of us would watch a couple of keystrokes every time someone logged on. You know, at someone's house or the computer lab." (You're not supposed to check your e-mail in computer lab, but everyone does it anyway.) "We kept a running list so that by halfway through the year, we had a lot of passwords."

"But all we ever do is read people's e-mails," Andy said very matter-of-factly. "We don't order them magazine subscriptions or anything like that."

"And you know Jonny's?" I asked.

"He was our test case," Andy said proudly.

"We read a couple of the e-mails you sent him," Walker admitted.

"And who else did you tell?" I asked.

"No one, I swear," Walker said.

"Then who would know to make the poster?"

I must've stumped them, because they both stared off into space searching for the answer.

"I guess it's possible that my older brother overheard me and Andy talking about it," Walker said.

"And then told all the other eighth graders?"

Walker winced, and all the pieces fell into place.

"We're really sorry, Caper," Andy said.

"Really sorry," Walker echoed. "And to prove it, I'm going to tell my mom on him."

"And the Principal!" I added.

Andy held out a folded up yellow sticky note. "For whatever it's worth, we got you something to make up for it."

"What's this?" I asked. "A paper time machine so we can go back and keep this from happening in the first place?"

"Just something we hope can help you," Andy said.

The bell suddenly rang, and the door flew open. Andy and Walker got washed away with the wave of students rushing into the building. I held my ground, and as the tide of students surged around me, I looked down at the paper and opened it up. There were four words scrawled in Andy's nearly illegible handwriting:

Screenname: serenabelle

Password: tennisgirl99

Andy and Walker had given me Serena Kingsley's e-mail password. Did that mean they weren't going to check her e-mail anymore? Or were they giving me the key to seeing what she may have written about me? The school day hadn't even officially started, and things were growing more complicated by the second.

Looking back, I have no idea how I made it through the day without my head exploding. I was pissed at Andy and Walker. I wanted to speak to Jonny but didn't even know how to begin to apologize. If it were up to me I would've cancelled Friday altogether. But Fridays I have computer lab, and there's no stopping the flow of data along the information superhighway. At least that's what our teacher, Dr. Patel, says.

As I sat at the computer, I glanced around and saw how easy it was for Andy and Walker to do their thing. Kids were checking their e-mails left and right instead of visiting the educational websites Dr. Patel had written on the board. I reached into my back pocket and used two fingers to carefully slide out my wallet. The problem with Velcro wallets is that they make a lot of noise when you open them, so I had to cough a couple of times to mask the sound. There was the paper with Serena's password—already curved to match my butt. My mind must have wandered off (which was becoming a dangerous habit) because Dr. Patel came over.

"Are you feeling all right, Mr. Speigelman?" he asked. "I am wondering if your blood sugar is getting low?"

I came out of my trance. Actually, I didn't feel low at all.

"No, I'm fine," I said. "I was just...uh...thinking about how amazing it is that I can retrieve information from any library in the world on any topic in the world through this computer."

Dr. Patel nodded knowingly. "Yes, yes, I agree," he said. "So why don't you retrieve some information about outer space instead of sitting here and staring off into it, hmm?"

The bell rang before too long, and we were off to lunch. At lunch on Fridays Jonny and I always get the pizza lunch that the PTA sells. But when lunch rolled around, I saw Jonny get on line first. I was sort of hoping to just slide back into our routine so we could pick up where we had left off on Wednesday. I guess Jonny had different plans. I got a rotten feeling in my stomach that stayed with me the rest of the day.

That night, I was going to check my e-mail but then I thought about my conversation with Andy and Walker and changed my mind. I went up to my room to focus my energy on one task and one task alone: my plan for dinner with Aunt Connie on Saturday night.

I dumped the stuff from the little white bag from the General Store onto my bed. I picked up the collar and pressed the cool metal studs against my fingertips. I must have been deep in thought, because I didn't even hear that distinctive knock at my door that usually sends me scrambling to barricade it. Whenever Lizzie comes to my room and the door

58

is closed, she has this way of dragging her knuckles down the door that drives me crazy. But, like I said, I didn't even know she was there until the door slowly creaked open. I dropped the collar and quickly flipped up my comforter to cover the evidence.

"Get out, Lizard," I said.

Lizzie padded inside on all fours. She was wearing black stretch pants, a black t-shirt, white gloves from her dress-up box, pointy black and white ears glued to a headband, and the belt from her bathrobe safety-pinned to her backside. Someone had used black eye makeup to draw whiskers, arching eyebrows and a little triangle nose.

"Me-ow," Lizzie purred. "Me-owwwww."

"What are you doing?" I asked, realizing as the words left my mouth that I really didn't care.

"I'm meow a kitty. I'm meow Mr. Whiskers."

"That's nice," I said. "Why don't you go use your litter box?"

Lizzie ignored me and crawled over, brushing up against my legs.

"Quit it!" I said. "And get out, Lizard-cat!"

"But I want to play kitty," she said. "We can play together."

"I don't think so," I said.

"Sure, you can be the doggie, and I'll be the kitty."

"I don't want to be—" And then I froze. "A what?"

"You already have the doggie collar," Lizzie said without a trace of accusation in her voice.

I casually glanced at the bed and saw that everything was completely hidden beneath the comforter. Then I thought back to Tuesday afternoon and replayed the events in my head. All the stuff was rolled up in the towel, except for the very tip of the leash. But even if she saw that tip of the leash, how would she know that I had a dog collar? Something was up.

"I don't know what you're talking about," I said, figuring the best thing to do was to deny, deny, deny.

"Pippa Rutledge told me that she saw you at the General Store buying doggie things," Lizzie said. "When Pippa asked if we had a doggie, I told her no, so she wanted to know why you bought all those doggie things."

I could feel my face getting a little hotter. So that's how she found out: that little rat Pippa Rutledge!

"So what did you tell her?" I asked Lizzie, trying my best to sound nonchalant.

"I told her I don't know why my stupid maniac brother does things," Lizzie said. "But I told her I thought it was because you are going to get a doggie some day and that you wanted to have the all the stuff ready just in case."

I was very impressed with Lizzie's answer, but I had to focus on getting anything to do with the dog stuff out of her head. I thought about saying that Pippa Rutledge couldn't remember what she had for breakfast much less what every person in the General Store bought. But I couldn't, because I knew that Pippa Rutledge was right and that her mother could back her up. So instead I said the thing that usually came to mind when I didn't want to deal with my sister:

"Get out of my room, Lizard!"

All the fun drained from Lizzie's face.

"Mommy made me this kitty face so I could play kitty and doggie with you," she pouted.

She said the magic word: "Mommy." I could not have her crying to our mom about this. I had to turn things around myself. And fast.

"Hold on, Lizard—I mean, Lizzie," I heard myself saying. Fortunately, thinking fast was a lot easier to do with Lizzie than with my parents. First, I would have to calm her down so she didn't do anything rash. I looked directly into her little brown eyes.

"Can you keep a secret?" I asked.

Her eyes widened as she nodded like an insane bobble-head doll.

"Okay, but you have to promise not to tell anyone," I said.

"I promise-promise."

"I bought all those things for a surprise," I said. "I'm going to dress up as a dog for Halloween, but no one can know. Last year when I told Mom and Dad my costume, they blabbed it to

61

all their friends who told their kids who then knew that I was going to be spaghetti and meatballs, and they all made fun of me so I ended up changing at the last minute to that ridiculous skeleton clown." (Which, by the way, wasn't at all true, because my friends and me decided not to do costumes for Halloween but then at the last minute, they all changed their minds so I had to pull together a costume and I got stuck using pieces of old costumes that didn't quite fit me anymore.)

Lizzie nodded. "Okay, I won't tell, Caper. Really." She gave me a pat on the shoulder and headed for the door. She stopped and turned around.

"What month is it?" she asked.

"May," I said.

"When's Halloween?" she asked.

I saw where this was going. "October."

"You're being very planful," she said with a smile and left.

I flopped backwards onto my bed and exhaled.

"The call was close," I said to myself. "Very, very close."

SATURDAY

When my mother knocked on my door, I could barely open my eyes. Then Lizzie burst in and jumped on my bed singing, "We're going to the diner! We're going to the diner!"

I looked at my clock. 9:30.

Lizzie bounced off my bed, out the door, and all the way down the stairs. Mom poked her head into the room. "Remember to test."

I hadn't been awake two minutes and already the nagging started. While I got dressed I realized how weird it was that we were going out for breakfast because we were also going out for dinner that night. I couldn't remember a single time in my entire life that we went out for two meals in the same day except on vacation and when we had no electricity for two days.

When I got downstairs I found out why. We'd run out of eggs, milk, bagels, frozen waffles, and just about every other conceivable breakfast food except for some instant oatmeal because Lizzie and Pippa Rutledge used it all up playing "Bed and Breakfast" with their dolls the day before.

Breakfast was uneventful except for the fight my dad got into with the manager over his "fork-split English muffin" that was actually split with a knife instead of a fork, shaving off all the nooks and crannies that are supposed to toast up all crispy and brown, which is what my father likes about English muffins.

When we got back, I saw Jonny riding his bike in figure-eights in front of my house. The rest of my family went inside, leaving me alone on the driveway.

I took a deep breath and cut across the lawn. Jonny pulled up to the curb.

"Hi," I said.

"Hi," he said. He handed me a shiny paper gift bag decorated with pictures of bulldozers and backhoes and dump trucks. "It was the only bag I could find in the house. I got you something to maybe help you out tonight. You know, sort of complete the ensemble."

I reached into the bag and pulled out something wrapped in newspaper. It was an odd shape, sort of rounded and scooped out. I peeled away the newspaper and smiled. In my hand I held a white plastic dog dish with the name "CAPER" written in Jonny-scrawl in black magic marker. A blue paw print decorated either side of my name.

"Thanks, Jonny," I said. "And I'm sorry about...you know, what I said." I couldn't bring myself to be any more specific than that, but Jonny understood.

"You know I'd never do anything like that," he said.

That made me feel even worse, but I had to take my medicine like a man. "Yeah, I know, me neither. And I'm really sorry."

Jonny nodded. "It really wasn't your fault. It was Andy and Walker."

There was a moment of awkward silence while I stuffed the bowl back into the bag.

"So...are you all set for tonight?"

"Getting there," I said. Another awkward pause followed. "Wanna shoot around?"

Jonny half-shrugged, half-nodded. We crossed the lawn to the hoop on the driveway. I opened the garage door and grabbed the ball.

We started a game of HORSE, and I caught him up on everything that had happened since I stopped speaking to him on Thursday. I started with a blow-by-blow from dinner Thursday when my fancy footwork and quick thinking saved the day and included everything up through Lizzie's cat craziness on Friday night. I was up H-O to Jonny's H-O-R-S when Jonny suddenly looked at me and smirked. It sort of unnerved me, and I missed my next shot. H-O-R for me.

"What is it?" I asked.

I passed the ball back to him. Jonny dribbled it a couple of times, stopped, turned sideways, and tried a hook shot with his right hand. It bounced on the rim and fell into the basket. I grabbed the ball and lined up the shot. Jonny looked at me and then raised his eyebrows in disbelief. I tried to act cool and pay no attention. I turned sideways and, as I raised my hand up to shoot, Jonny said,

"Nothing...except for one tiny detail that can bring your plans crashing to the ground."

A mild wave of panic washed over me as the ball left my hand. The ball ricocheted off the backboard and onto my front yard. H-O-R-S. As I ran after the ball, I frantically replayed in my mind everything I told him about but couldn't find anything wrong.

"What are you talking about?" I shouted. "I didn't reveal anything–"

"Shhhhhh!" Jonny said, waving his arms around to remind me that the entire neighborhood could hear what I was saying. My voice dropped to a whisper.

"–anything about my plan, and at dinner I was able to distract them all from the whole General Store visit with incredibly quick thinking." I passed the ball to Jonny, maybe a little too hard because he went "Ooof" when he caught it. He dribbled, took two steps, and launched the basketball. It slapped against the backboard and dropped through the net. I rebounded and dribbled over to where Jonny stood and took his position. As I focused on the net, I could see Jonny nodding his head.

"I can't believe you don't remember what you told your parents Thursday night," he added without a trace of judgment in his voice.

I didn't want to give him another chance to throw me off my game, so I moved quickly. I took the two steps, and just as I began my motion to release the ball, Jonny half whispered,

"You told them you were at the General Store buying Lizzie a present!"

The ball left my hand with some kind of funky spin on it. It hit the backboard, dropped to the rim, and then rolled around the outside of the rim before falling to the ground. He was right. I'd completely forgotten I told them that when I was at the General Store getting my dog stuff I was really buying a present for The Lizard.

"That's E!" he said, scooping up the ball and sending off a shot in a single fluid motion. The ball soared gracefully and dropped right through the basket.

"Nothing but net!" he declared triumphantly.

"Great. Now get me a shovel," I said.

"Why?"

"Cause I seem to keep digging myself out of one hole and into another."

We laughed and went inside. We found two glasses of water on the counter. I also noticed that my blood testing kit was conveniently placed next to one of the glasses.

"How subtle," I mumbled. I took a few big gulps, making as much noise as possible. Jonny heard me and started laughing with his mouthful of water. He choked and spit out his water, spraying it all over counter. I burst into laughter. He laughed harder and started coughing, his eyes bugging out of his head, which only made me laugh harder.

We finally cleaned up the mess, and Jonny said he had to go. "Why don't you ride with me via downtown?"

"Great idea!" I said. "Dad? Mom? I'm going to ride Jonny home!"

My mother's voice echoed all the way from upstairs and into the kitchen.

"Did you test?" she yelled back.

Uch! I stopped in my tracks and realized I had forgotten to test when we came inside. I stomped back towards the counter and opened my kit. I did it as quickly as I could and as soon as I heard the double beep, I shouted my number back to my mother.

"Ninety-three!" Only my mother wasn't upstairs anymore. She was standing in the kitchen.

"What was that dear, I didn't hear you?"

I instantly felt terrible. I know that my mom only nags me because she loves me, and I know that my mother's always worried about me, and I know that I shouldn't be fresh when it comes to my diabetes. But it's really hard when everything you do is watched and recorded and you can't just do whatever you want just because you feel like it.

On the other hand, I think sometimes it's a lot easier to actually have a disease like diabetes than have to take care of someone who has it. I know it's a weird thing to say, but I don't think I put nearly as much energy into worrying about my highs and lows as my parents do, and my mother in particular. I just go about my business and do my thing. My mother is the one who stays on top of schedules and supplies and makes charts and lists and tracks glucose and insulin and all that. And when I really think about it, I realize that the only way I can be so relaxed about things is because my mother isn't. So I have to cut her some slack sometimes, you know?

"Sorry for yelling," I said, adding to my defense, "but I thought you were still upstairs."

Mom smiled. "I know, dear. You're just riding to Jonny's and back?"

She gave me a look, and I knew exactly what she wasn't saying: you're not going to pull what you pulled the other day after school, are you? Moms and their radar. But I really didn't want to lie again, so I didn't...not completely.

"Yeah," I answered. "But we may go through town first because Jonny wants to get something for Eric and wants my help picking it out."

I know, I'm a bad friend for dragging Jonny into my lie. But it's really his fault for pointing out that I needed to get something for Lizzie.

"Fine," she said. "Ride safely."

We helmeted up and pedaled off down the street. We didn't get more than a hundred yards when I slammed on the brakes.

"What's the matter?" Jonny asked.

"I forgot my wallet," I said.

"We'll stop at my house and get mine," he said.

We rode up into his driveway. Jonny jumped off his bike and ran inside. He came out a second later, stuffing something into his pocket. His brother Eric tagged along, also wearing his helmet.

"Wait for me!" Eric shouted. "I want to go too! Can I come?" Jonny's mother followed about ten paces behind Eric. At exactly the same time that Jonny said, "NO!" his mother said, "YES!"

At that moment, I felt Jonny's pain. I couldn't count how many times I had to drag The Lizard along with me somewhere. It was nice to know I wasn't the only one. I realized that having Eric along for this particular errand wouldn't be such a big deal. I flicked Jonny on the back of his arm to get his attention. When he turned to me, I shrugged. That was the international big brother signal for "it really doesn't matter if he comes or not because we both know your brother is so insignificant that you may as well let him come and save your fight for another time."

Jonny sighed and said, "Fine, Eric, let's go."

Eric ran back to get his bike while Jonny and I rode in circles in the street.

"Race to the fifth pole!" I announced. Jonny and I took off but Eric, being a couple of years younger, had a smaller bicycle and wasn't able to keep up. Unlike Lizzie, he didn't stop to cry about it. He pumped his legs and did his best to keep pace.

Jonny happened to live down the block from Serena, and as we rode past her house, I glanced in that direction. Big mistake. My front tire hit a small rock, and by the time I turned forward, I felt my momentum shifting. My front wheel turned slightly to the right and I had the sensation of the street being pulled out from under me. A second later, I was down, but fortunately, I was on the grass. Unfortunately, it was Serena's grass. Jonny double-backed while Eric had just caught up.

"You okay, Caper?" Jonny asked.

"Yeah," I nodded, standing up. My jeans were torn below the right knee and sported some pretty intense grass stains, but otherwise they looked fine. My knee itself stung a little. I picked up my bike, throwing another glance over my shoulder at Serena's house. I wondered if she was in there at that moment, looking out at me and thinking, "What a looooser!"

I got back on my bike and the three of us rode a little more slowly into town. My right knee was definitely sore, but I wasn't about to make a big deal about it. We parked our bikes out in front, and once in the General Store, I went directly to the rack of stuffed animals.

"Hey, Jonny, what's my budget?" I asked.

Jonny pulled a wad of crumpled bills from his pocket and counted.

"About one, two, three, four, five, six dollars...and ten, twenty, thirty, five, forty, five, fifty, five...six, seven...six dollars and fifty seven cents."

I spun the rack around, closed my eyes, and waited for it stop. I opened my eyes and saw a flamingo. I looked at the price tag: $5.95.

"Bingo!"

Jonny and I went to the cash register. The cashier had her back to us, putting something away on the shelves behind the counter. Eric's hand reached up and rang the little bell sitting next to the register. The cashier slowly turned around, and as she did another bell rang, but this time in my head. It was Mrs. Sweeney who was there the day I bought the dog stuff. Not wanting her to see me, I spun around myself as if I absolutely had to see the exciting things for sale on the rack beside the front counter. But I sort of turned a little too much and came face to face with the people standing behind me: Serena and Mary. Serena pursed her lips and stared at me through steely green eyes.

"Well, if isn't Caper," Mary said, crossing her arms and raising her right eyebrow. I was not getting a good feeling from either of them. Frozen, I smiled, nodded, and made a sound that was half "Hi" and half seal-bark.

"What's wrong with your voice?" Mary asked, never one to mince words. I felt my cheeks getting hot until I thought they were going to melt right off my skull.

"Nothing," I said.

"Whatcha up to?" Serena asked. I noticed Mary peering over my shoulder at what Jonny was buying. I pointed over my shoulder at Jonny, who was just finishing. Eric came over and announced for everyone in the General Store to hear that I had wiped out on her lawn.

I wanted to grab Eric by the shoulders and shake him until his eyeballs rolled back into his head and out of his mouth. But that was out of the question. Instead, I shot him a mean look that he didn't even see because he had already moved on to the magazine rack where there were several issues of his favorite skateboarding magazines.

"Really?" Mary asked. "I wonder if that's something I'd read about in an e-mail."

I had no idea where that came from.

"I don't know," I shrugged.

"Because if someone did write about it in an e-mail, it would be private, wouldn't it?" Mary added. She sounded like a lawyer on one of those trial shows. "And when something's private, no one else is supposed to read it, are they?"

"No," I said, still not sure where this was going. I glanced back at Jonny trying to will him to move more quickly.

"That's right, e-mails are private and personal things, Caper Spiegelman," Mary said.

"What are you talking about?" I asked.

"Skip told me everything," Mary said. "Everything about you and your cruddy friends Andy and Walker and your little password game."

The pieces instantly fell into place, but before I could get anything out, Serena looked at me, but this time the corners of her mouth drooped and her eyes looked away.

"I'm really disappointed," was all she said. She and Mary turned and left.

"And consider yourself uninvited to my party," Mary threw over her shoulder.

"But...I didn't...I mean..." No matter how hard I tried, I couldn't make the words come out the way I wanted them to. It was almost like that dream where I tried to talk but couldn't. Except that this wasn't a dream at all. With Serena walking away, shaking her head like that, it was more like a nightmare.

When I got home with my present for Lizzie, she was in the kitchen snacking on baby carrots. I blew right past her without so much as a "hello" and went right to the stairs. Had I been paying attention, I would have seen her examining the outside of a small bag covered with construction vehicles that was sitting on the kitchen counter. Only when I heard her shout, "Mommy! Is this bag for me?" did the alarms go off inside my head. I immediately backtracked to the kitchen and snatched the bag off the counter.

"HEY!" Lizzie cried.

"That's mine," I said.

"I found it first!" Lizzie whined. "It's mine, you maniac! Now give it to me or I'm telling Mom!"

For as slowly as my brain had been working the past few days, my hands more than made up for it. While Lizzie cried and moaned, I held the gift bag behind my back and somehow managed to dump the stuffed animal into it and move the dog dish into my General Store bag.

"MOMMY! DADDY!" Lizzie yelled, her face beet red, her eyes filling up with water.

My parents ran into the kitchen from different parts of the house to see what I'm sure they thought would be some new form of torture I had devised for my sister. What they saw instead was me handing Lizzie the construction vehicle gift bag.

"Here. It was supposed to be a surprise, but you ruined it with your whining babyness."

Lizzie's eyes lit up.

"You mean it really *is* for me?" she asked. If you ask me, I think she believed that wanting it to be for her was enough to make it actually be for her. Lizzie reached into the bag and pulled out the tiny stuffed flamingo.

"Cool," she said, examining it from all sides. "What is it?"

"A flamingo," I said.

She studied it and nodded.

"I'm going to call him Phil," she declared. "Phil the flamingo! Now I'm going to introduce him to all my other animals. Thankscaperyourethegreatestbye." She jumped off the counter stool and ran straight upstairs. My parents looked at me and smiled.

"That was very nice, Caper," Mom said. "Lizzie's very lucky to have a brother like you." She came over and gave me a big hug. She heard the plastic bag rustle. "What's in the bag?"

I didn't want to dig myself into another hole, so I told the truth...mostly.

"It's something, uh, for tonight," I said. "A surprise."

"Can't wait," Mom said.

"And we're leaving at six o'clock on the dot," Dad said. "Not five after six. When you go upstairs, tell your sister."

On my way out of the kitchen, I noticed a folded-up piece of paper on the floor. It must have fallen out of the gift bag when I switched the dog dish for the flamingo. I opened the note:

Good luck tonight. Remember to stand firm, be aggressive, and if all else fails, sit up and beg. Jonny

I laughed and put the note in my pocket. My day so far had been full of ups and downs, but Jonny's note gave me the boost I needed to earn my big brother points for the day. When I got upstairs, I opened Lizzie's door and stuck my head inside. She was sitting on her bed with an enormous pile of stuffed animals, introducing Phil to each one of them.

"Hey, Lizzie, Dad says we're leaving at 6:30, so take your time."

I closed the door and smiled. Sometimes it's fun being a big brother.

The place we were going for dinner wasn't very fancy, but since my aunt was coming, I had to wear a pair of nice pants and a shirt with a collar. I wasn't happy about it because I was worried that the shirt collar would take away from the full impact of my dog collar. So I decided to wear a t-shirt underneath my collared shirt. I rifled through my drawer and pulled out an old tie-dyed tank top Dad brought back from one of his business trips.

I got dressed and stood in front of my mirror. I wish I had a camera for a "Before" and "After" shot. I tried to imagine what I'd look like in all my dog regalia but was interrupted by my father's voice shouting, "Five minutes!"

I stuffed my collar, leash and bandana into an old backpack. On my way out the door, I remembered the supper dish and grabbed that too, shoving it into my bag. As I walked downstairs, I heard my mother coming out of her room. She knocked on Lizzie's door and then opened it up.

"Elizabeth Taylor Speigelman!" Mom yelled. "We're leaving in five minutes and you're not even dressed yet?!" I heard Lizzie began to protest but then the door closed and all I heard was some muffled shouting and then some crying.

In the kitchen, I grabbed a testing kit and tossed it into my bag. It was 5:59 PM K.C.T. (that's Kitchen Clock Time, the official time of the Speigelman family), and Dad was ready to go. When the clock struck 6:00, my Dad shouted, "Six o'clock! Time to leave! Where is everybody?"

"Just a minute, Aaron!" my mother called back. "We'll be right down!"

At 6:04, my father yelled upstairs again. This time, my mother ignored him, which was her way of telling him to back off. Finally, Mom stomped down the stairs dragging Lizzie and Phil behind.

"Can we go now?" my father asked.

"Absolutely," Mom replied.

"Then let's go! We're already behind schedule. I don't want to be late for our reservation."

"I think we'll be fine, honey," Mom said. "Caper, do you have—"

"Yeah, I've got my kit," I replied, tapping my backpack.

"Fine, you can test at the restaurant," she said.

"Are we picking Aunt Connie up at the bus stop?" asked Lizzie.

"No, she's meeting us there," my dad grunted as he backed the car out of the driveway. "She's getting a ride."

It wasn't until Lizzie mentioned Aunt Connie's name that I began to wonder what her surprise could be.

The drive was pretty boring, except when we got stuck behind a bus and my father almost had a stroke every time it stopped. When we finally got to the restaurant, Dad reminded us to take everything we needed with us as if the car was going to be parked in Russia instead of just outside the restaurant.

"And Lizzie, your pelican has to stay in the car. They don't allow pelicans in the restaurant," he said.

"Flamingo!" Lizzie said, clutching her new friend tightly. "Phil's a flamingo!"

My father sighed. "Sorry, my mistake. Just don't let anyone see him."

"Why not?"

As we walked into the restaurant I whispered, "I hear they've got this new chef who's been dying to try out a recipe for flamingo soup."

Lizzie stuffed Phil beneath her sweater.

We checked in at the hostess station and were told our table would be ready in about fifteen minutes. I passed the time inside my head, walking through my plan and, more importantly, all of the clever things I was going to say. When the hostess finally called out, "Spiegelman, party of six!" I shot out of my chair like a rocket.

We followed the hostess through the crowded restaurant, and I quickly counted the members of my family: Mom, Dad, me and The Lizard. That made four, plus Aunt Connie was five. Where did six come from? Maybe the hostess got it wrong, I thought. Maybe they were putting us at a table for six since we were too many to fit at the table for four. That had happened plenty of times before. We followed the hostess to the back room and to a round table in the corner. It was set for six, so I decided to do what I'd seen Dad do at other restaurants.

"We're only five, so you can take this place setting," I said, pointing to the seat in front of me.

"Actually, we are six," Mom said. "But thanks, sweetie."

We weren't at the table ten seconds and already my mother embarrassed me. My cheeks quickly flushed, and I sat down without a word. I could tell that no one else was really interested in why there were six of us instead of five. Lizzie was too busy checking on Phil, making sure he could breathe beneath her sweater. My parents picked up their menus, and I heard my aunt's voice.

"Well, they'll let anyone into this place, won't they?"

"Aunt Connie!" Lizzie cheered, knocking over her chair as she leaped into our aunt's arms. I had clearly missed the "let's embarrass Caper" memo that everyone else in my family obviously got. Phil fell to the floor and Lizzie panicked.

"Oh no!" she cried. "Phil!" She squirmed out of Aunt Connie's arms and grabbed the flamingo. Lizzie ran back to her seat and sank down.

"Hi, Aaron, Hi, Randie," Aunt Connie said to my folks, giving each a kiss on the cheek. Then she turned to me. "Hey,

Cape!" As she bent down and gave me a kiss, I noticed my father looking towards the door.

"Is your ride coming in?" he asked.

"Left something in the car," Aunt Connie replied, sitting down in the empty chair to my right. Lizzie was to my left, and my father was next to her. That left the other empty seat between Mom and Aunt Connie. So now it was beginning to make sense. A friend of Aunt Connie's had given her a ride and was going to stay for dinner. With that mystery solved, I was dying to ask her about the surprise.

"Hit any traffic coming out?" my father asked. The man was obsessed with traffic.

"Just a little back-up on the bridge," Aunt Connie said.

Mom glanced towards the door and nudged my aunt. I looked up and saw a man walking towards us. He must have been over six feet tall! He was wearing a black sport coat and a black shirt with thin grey squiggles on it. I thought he was the waiter or something, but when he got to the table, Aunt Connie stood up and put her hand behind his back.

"Everyone, this is Simon," she announced. "Simon, this is my brother, Aaron, and his wife, Randie." Dad stood up and shook Simon's hand. Dad gave solid handshakes, and often told me that a person's first impression comes from a handshake. I remember spending a whole afternoon once practicing my handshake. Dad and Simon exchanged "Nice to meet you's." Mom offered her hand without standing, and Simon shook it as well. Then Aunt Connie turned to me and Lizzie.

"This is my adorable niece, Lizzie," Aunt Connie said. Lizzie looked up.

"Hi, Lizzie!" Simon said, his voice sounding friendly.

Lizzie stared at him and said, "You're not a chef, are you?"

Mom looked at Dad and shook her head. Simon smiled and shook his head.

"No, I'm a teacher," he replied.

"Good," Lizzie said. "Because no one's going to put Phil in the soup!"

"And no one should! Why, that would be just awful if someone put Phil in the soup!" Simon agreed. "Who's Phil?"

Lizzie looked around to make sure no one was looking. She very quickly took Phil out, showed him to Simon, and then stuffed him back under her sweater. Aunt Connie looked at my parents. Mom shook her head and shrugged.

"And you must be Caper," Simon said, finally sitting down. He extended his hand. For some reason, I felt this was the moment that I had been practicing all those handshakes for. So I reached out and watched my hand basically disappear into Simon's enormous paw. I gave the firmest handshake I could, holding it for a full three-count, just like Dad had taught me.

"Good grip, Caper," Simon said, releasing me. Then he leaned in close and whispered, "You can tell a lot about a man by his handshake."

And that's when my body decided to join in on the "let's embarrass Caper" fun. As I pulled my hand back, it flopped sideways and knocked over Aunt Connie's water glass. The water leaped out of the glass, barely glancing over the tablecloth as it streamed right onto Simon's lap!

A chorus of "Oh my!" and "Are you okay?" and "Caper!" and who knows what else filled my ears. I felt the blood surge to my cheeks. All I wanted to do was run to the bathroom and stuff my head into the toilet to douse the flames that engulfed my face, ears, and the rest of my humiliated self. I could see Aunt Connie's pinched expression, and for the first time I saw a resemblance between her and my father.

I mumbled an apology (or at least I think I did), and Simon replied, "That's all right, Caper, I needed to wash these pants anyway. You saved me a trip to the cleaners."

That's when about half the waiters in the restaurant surrounded our table and performed their famous Tablecloth Switch Ballet. I had actually heard about it from Jonny and Andy, who both witnessed it first-hand. It was one of those things that Happy Clammy's was famous for. In a perfectly-timed set of maneuvers, three waiters scooped up our place settings while two more grabbed the other stuff. Another waiter whisked the wet tablecloth away while another placed a new on one the table. The plates and stuff went back on the table and in less than a minute everything was good as new.

"Impressive," Simon said. "They should take that act on the road."

I couldn't bear to sit there for another minute. "I'm going to test," I said, grabbing my bag.

"Okay, dear," Mom replied.

I walked away from the table and heard Simon call, "Hold up, Caper. I'll join you."

I kept walking and Simon caught up to me. The last thing I wanted was to be with the person I just dumped a glass of water on. When we got to the bathroom, Simon's arm reached out over me and pushed the door open. I went straight into a stall.

"So you're in sixth grade, Caper, right?" he asked. I heard the "whummmmmp" of the paper towel dispenser, and I pictured Simon trying to dry off his pants. "I teach eighth grade math. You know, algebra and pre-algebra, that sort of stuff."

It was weird. I mean talking to Jonny in the bathroom was one thing because, you know, we have things to talk about. But I didn't even know this guy, and here he was talking to me while I was supposed to be peeing or something? Totally gross.

So I didn't answer. But not wanting to be completely rude, I made sort of a "hmmm" sound.

I heard the urinal flush, and then the sink, and then the "whummmmmmp" of the paper towel dispenser again. I thought Simon was done, but for some reason he didn't leave. He stood in front of the mirror by the sinks for another minute. His cell phone beeped a couple of times and then I heard his footsteps move across the floor.

"See you back at the table, Caper," he said on the way out. When I heard the door close, I unlocked the stall, put my bag on the counter, and tested my blood. I looked at the stuff in my bag for some quick encouragement. I quickly glanced in the mirror and saw something I wasn't expecting: the look of fear.

I shook it off and said, "You da dog!"

When I got back, there were two baskets of bread and a platter of meat, smelly cheese and oil-soaked vegetables on the table.

"We're all ready to order, Caper," Mom said. "So take a look and see what you want."

I opened the menu and looked it over. I usually got chicken parmesan, but I thought I'd try something different.

"What can I get for you this evening?" the waitress asked, looking at Mom. Mom ordered, followed by Aunt Connie. Then the waitress looked at Lizzie. "And how about you, young lady?"

"Buttered noodles," Lizzie said. "And a meatball. Please."

"What kind of noodles would you like, dear?" the waitress asked.

Lizzie put on her thinking face and pondered the waitress's question.

"Do you have bow ties?" she asked.

The waitress said, "You bet," and wrote something on her pad.

"Good," Lizzie said. "I'll have the tubies, please,"

"I thought you wanted bow ties," Mom said.

"No, I just wanted to know if they had them," Lizzie replied. "I like the tubies."

The waitress scribbled on her pad and wrote something else. Then she looked at me.

"Yes, I'll have the twin lobster tails and petit sirloin," I said.

Well, you'd think I'd ordered everything on the menu because before the waitress could put pen to paper, my father erupted.

"WHOOOOOOAAAAA! Hold on there, sport!"

I looked up as if I had no idea what he was talking about.

"Why don't you try something else?" Dad suggested. I could tell by how his eyebrows were inching up over his forehead that my choice was not very popular with him. Totally embarrassed, I slammed the menu down and said, "Fine! Chicken parmesan."

"Please..." my mother added.

"Please," I said, looking up at the waitress.

The waitress took Dad's and Simon's orders and then our menus. Aunt Connie leaned over Simon and whispered something to my mother. Simon leaned back and tapped me on the shoulder.

"Good call on the lobster tail, Caper," he said. "That was my first choice too, but since you're dad's paying, I didn't want to go overboard." He winked at me and then sat back.

I wished I could have told him how lame he sounded, but I knew that would've just made everyone mad. And that comment of his was just the beginning. For the whole meal he kept asking me questions about school and sports and movies and stuff that I really didn't want to talk about since all I wanted to do was figure out when I was going to make my move but I couldn't do that if Simon wouldn't stop talking so at one point I starting saying to myself, "Please shut up shut up shut up shut up shut up SHUT UP!"

That's when the restaurant become eerily quiet and I realized that everyone was staring at me. I actually said it out loud!

"Caper!" Dad said, his half-whispered voice dripping with anger.

"Um...sorry," I said, my cheeks reaching their boiling point. "I was...um...thinking of a...joke that Jonny told me and...I uh..."

"Must've been one heckuva joke," Simon said. "So anyway, as I was saying..." and then he jumped right back into the middle of a conversation with my parents and Aunt Connie and that was it. My parents didn't even have a chance to yell at me or anything because Simon scooped up their attention. So maybe Simon wasn't so bad, but I wasn't going to let him ruin my plans. In fact, I decided at that instant that it was time.

"I'm going to the bathroom," I said, grabbing my backpack and standing up.

"I have to go too!" Lizzie said as she jumped up.

Dang! I could not take Lizzie with me! Not now!

"Great, so do I," Aunt Connie said. "Let's go, Lizzie. And don't forget Phil."

Aunt Connie, Lizzie and I walked together to the bathrooms. For a moment, it felt like old times.

"So what do you think, Caper?" Aunt Connie asked.

"About what?" I said.

"About my surprise," she said.

"I don't know. It depends on what it is."

Aunt Connie laughed. "Caper, Simon is the surprise," she said. "He's my boyfriend. We've been seeing each other for a while now, and this is the first time he's meeting anyone in my family. This is a pretty big night for him. For us."

"Oh," I said. I wanted Aunt Connie to be happy, because I was going to need her on my side. But I also didn't want to lie, because even though he seemed nice, Simon was a bit of a dork as far as I was concerned. So I thought and came up with the best I could.

"He seems cool...for a math teacher."

Aunt Connie smiled. I guess that was good enough.

"He was dying to meet you, Caper," she said. "I told him all about you. You know, you two have a lot in common."

I wanted to ask if he was named after a dog also, but Lizzie interrupted.

"Aunt Connie, I have to go..." she whined.

Aunt Connie laughed again. "Ooops, sorry, Lizzie, let's go." They went into the Ladies' Room and I went into the Men's Room. I wondered what she meant by "You two have a lot in common" but only until I locked myself in a stall and opened my backpack.

I draped the leash, collar and bandana on the hook on the stall door. I took off my shirt, and as I did I suddenly felt very exposed even though I was wearing the tie-dye shirt underneath. It just felt weird taking off my shirt in a public bathroom. I quickly looked around to see if there were any security cameras. There weren't. Next I took off my belt and stuffed it into my bag with my shirt.

I took the leash and weaved it through my belt loops. I put the collar on but had trouble fastening it because my hands were shaking. I was either getting super low or super nervous. Since I had just eaten, I knew I couldn't be low, so it must have been nerves. I opened the stall door and used the mirror over the sinks to help me see how to fasten the collar properly. I tried a few different things for the bandana and settled on tying it in a triangle around my neck, making sure it was loose enough to hang below the dog collar.

The bathroom door creaked open. An old man shuffled into the bathroom and went right into a stall. He didn't even notice me. He locked the door and farted like he was completely deflating. The stench was so bad I felt pieces of dinner reaching up from my stomach, and I knew I had to get out of there. I shoved all my stuff into my backpack and studied my reflection.

What I was about to do was probably the most dangerous thing I'd ever done, and probably the last thing I'd ever do if my parents killed me, which was a distinct possibility considering the amount of embarrassment I was about to cause. My hands were shaking, and my heartbeat was all jittery. My stomach knew this was a bad idea. My brain knew this was bad idea. The insulin and carbo duking it out in my blood knew this was a bad idea. But I didn't care. My course was set. My path was clear. I took a deep breath and kicked open the bathroom door. That's when I remembered that the door opened inward. So after hopping around for a few moments with a stubbed foot, I reached out and yanked the door open. I stepped out into the heart of the Saturday night dinner crowd at Happy Clammy's.

I kind of wish I had a camera with me because I would have loved to capture this moment on film. Everyone's eyes started falling on me, but I fixed my gaze straight ahead and focused all of my energy on remaining calm. I walked towards the table, reminding myself to breathe slowly. My ears tingled and my cheeks flushed as some folks laughed, some pointed, some just stared, and others looked up and went back to their meals. But I didn't care. At least I didn't care until I made eye contact with the one other familiar face in the restaurant: Serena Kingsley.

My heart jumped into my throat, then dropped back into my chest, then back up to my neck, and continued yo-yo-ing as I passed her table. I smiled ever so slightly at her but otherwise kept my eyes focused straight ahead of me. Like a shark, I had to keep moving forward or I knew I'd die. As I approached our table at the back of the restaurant, I saw that Lizzie and Aunt Connie were already in their seats. Lizzie noticed me right away.

"Caper's wearing his Halloween costume! I want to wear my Halloween costume! That's not fair!"

That was not how I wanted things to begin, but there was no turning back. Mom, Dad, Aunt Connie and Simon turned and watched me come back to the table. I was still playing it cool, like nothing was different about me. So when I got to the table I sat down and put my napkin on my lap.

"Did we order dessert?"

Then I went to Phase Two. I took the dog dish Jonny had given me out of my bag and put it in the empty space where my plate had been. I emptied my water glass into the dish, leaned forward and began to lap up the water...just like a dog! It was then that I discovered that I really wasn't much of a dog. My tongue wasn't long enough to pick up the water, so I had to put almost my whole face into the dish to get any. And when I did start lapping it up, my nose got wet and most of the water I lapped up ran down my chin, under the dog collar, and onto my bandana and shirt. There was nothing at all pleasant or thirst-quenching about it, but I couldn't stop, because I had a point to make.

When I picked my head up, my parents looked at me like I had six heads. I had never seen those kinds of expressions on their faces before. Dad's mouth hung open and Mom's lips were all puckered up like she swallowed a lemon. And true to form, Lizzie ruined it

"I want my Halloween costume! It's no fair that Caper gets to wear his!"

"Caper...?" Mom said, not quite knowing what else to say.

"Yes?" I replied.

"Any particular reason you felt it necessary to dress up like a dog?" Dad asked, somewhat off-handedly, like he was asking someone why they had ordered pea soup instead chicken soup.

Well, this was the moment I had been waiting for. This was the set-up, my chance to finally bring it all out into the open. I had thought about different ways of saying it. I had rehearsed the conversation in my mind over and over and over until I thought I had played out every possibility. I had an entire list of well-reasoned responses, sarcastic remarks, and biting comments at the ready.

But as soon as my father asked the question for real, my brain froze. It was like all of the words lined up in my mind lost their grip and tumbled down from my brain, through my body, and into my feet where they lay in a jumbled, leaden heap, leaving nothing but a vast blankness behind.

And without those words, my well-crafted defenses crumbled and my heart began pounding like a gorilla typing on computer keyboard. It pounded and pounded, shooting out words and sending them up to my brain. But unlike the original words that were carefully crafted, these words were wild and full of terrible, hateful emotions. They rushed up with such force that I felt them swimming around my head, pushing up against my face from the inside. There was so much pressure building the water swelled up from my eyes. My throat tightened, making it hard to swallow. I wanted so badly to push those words back down but I couldn't because my heart kept surging them forward with such force I felt myself drowning in them.

My brain struggled to force back those terrible words while at the same time trying to make sense of what was happening around me. I looked at my parents and saw their worried expressions and Aunt Connie who tried to smile and Simon who sat there holding an insulin pump just like mine and why did he have my pump and wait a second it wasn't my pump because I was wearing my pump and the tube went into his body and it was *his* pump and that means the beeping I had heard in the bathroom wasn't his cell phone it was his blood glucose meter and oh my Simon's diabetic and that's what Aunt Connie meant when she said we had stuff in common and that was her surprise for me!

And while the heart-words and brain-words collided inside me I wanted to scream because I thought that was the only way to release the pressure but the more I tried to speak the harder it was and more tears were running down my face than I could ever remember and those terrible, hateful thoughts finally forced their way out of my mouth.

"Great, that's just what this family needs, another diabetic freak like me!"

I jumped up and ran through the restaurant, knocking past waiters and the people waiting for their tables. I blasted through the front door and darted across the parking lot. One of the valets stopped short to avoid hitting me. I ran through the lot and dropped to the ground behind a black car in the furthest corner. I cried like I hadn't cried since I was like two or three and the next thing I knew Aunt Connie was crouching next to me. She didn't say anything, but I felt her hand rubbing circles on my back.

I tried to regain control of my breathing. My throat ached and still felt tight. I pulled my knees up against my chest and rest my chin on them. The last thing I could do was look at anyone, so I stared at the grass that edged the corner of the parking lot.

"Caper..." Aunt Connie said, "can your parents come over?"

I didn't know. I didn't care. So I shrugged.

"Do you want me to stay?" she asked.

That I did know. And I did care. So I nodded.

My parents must have been right there, only I didn't see them until that moment. My folks knelt down on either side of me. My mom wrapped me in her arms, but I kept myself tucked in. My dad put his hand on my shoulder.

"Caper," Mom whispered. "Caper, Caper...we love you."
She kissed me on my head. Now I was beginning to get a little
self-conscious. The tears were done and the full impact of what
had just happened was beginning to sink in.

"Do you feel all right?" Mom asked. "Are you feeling low?"

There it was again, diabetes getting in the way of my life.
And I felt a new surge of anger and resentment well up.

"I feel fine!" I said, pulling away. "You know, Mom, not
everything's about my diabetes!"

"Based on what you said to Simon, I'm not so sure," Dad
said.

Simon. I gasped. I said a terrible thing to Simon. It was a
horrible rotten thing to say and all of the anger that had just
come back dissolved into guilt and sadness. I looked up at
Aunt Connie who was wiping her crying eye.

"I'm really sorry, Aunt Connie, I didn't mean anything by
it," I said, tears filling my eyes again. A few drops streamed
down my cheeks before I was able to shut the faucet off again.

"I know, sweetie," she smiled. "You know, Simon's been
diabetic since he was two. He's a great guy, and I think you two
could really get along well. He said he'd be happy to talk to you
whenever you wanted. He understands, Caper. He understands
in a way that me, Mom and Dad never will."

I stood up and gave her a hug.

"It's just...it's just so hard," I said into her shoulder. She hugged me then grabbed my shoulders and pushed me back.

"Now then, Caper, what's with the dog show?" she asked.

I took that as a signal from her that it was okay for me to break my promise and confront my parents about you-know-what. I turned to face my folks.

"You want to know why I'm dressed like this, don't you?" I asked them.

"The question had crossed our minds," Dad said.

"It's because I know."

My folks looked at me, waiting for me to finish the sentence.

"Know what, dear?" asked Mom.

I took a deep breath and said those fateful words. "I know that you named me after your dog."

"Oh," Mom said. She didn't look the least bit worried, concerned...or sorry. I glanced at Aunt Connie, whose expression had morphed into one of eye-bulging horror. She covered her mouth with her hand and shook her head slowly from side to side, as if to say, "No, Caper, don't do it! DON'T DO IT!" But I had come too far and there was no turning back.

"Mom, Dad, Aunt Connie told me how you had a whole other name for me but decided at the last minute to name me after your dog."

Mom, Dad, and Aunt Connie looked at each other.

"That certainly puts things in perspective," Dad said. "But there's just one thing."

"Yeah?" I asked.

Mom looked at Dad and back at me.

"We didn't name you after a dog," she said.

"What?" I said.

"We didn't name you after a dog."

"But Aunt Connie said..." I began, but my father turned and faced his sister.

"Your Aunt Connie told you that?" he said, sounding a lot more interested in *how* I found out than in *what* I found out.

"Yeah, but that's only because that's what you told me!" Aunt Connie protested.

My dad's eyes nearly popped out of his skull. "WHAT?!"

"Caper, now listen," Mom said. "You father and I most certainly did NOT name you after a dog. We named you after my Great Uncle Charlie, like we told you. But if you want to know the truth, we did have another name for you picked out. After you were born though we had a chance to watch your tiny little baby arms and legs kicking and fluttering like you were in a hurry to get somewhere. And we realized the name we had chosen didn't fit at all. So your father came up with something that reflected your spirit."

I listened and nodded. "What was the first name?"

My father looked at me. "Patricia."

"What?!" It was Aunt Connie's turn now to be caught off guard.

"We never told anyone, but the doctor was positive you were going to be a girl," Dad explained.

"Well, better to give him a dog's name than a girl's name, I suppose," Aunt Connie said.

"Connie, there was no dog!" Dad said, obviously irritated with his little sister. At that moment, I heard my own voice in Dad's.

"Aaron, she's talking about the McCovey's dog," Mom said. "Remember that winter we dog-sat for them while they were in Europe? The little white dog? That got snow-plowed? His name was Lincoln? Stop me if any of this sounds familiar."

"Lincoln? You told me the dog's name was Caper!" Aunt Connie said.

Mom turned and glared at Dad. "Really?"

A spark of recognition suddenly flashed in my father's eyes as a long-forgotten memory suddenly exploded inside his head.

"Huh," was all he said at first. His mind sort of drifted away for a moment as I guess he relived the whole scene inside his head. "I was just trying the name on for size."

"On a dog?!" Mom replied. It was becoming clear to me that my little episode back in the restaurant was no longer the focus of everyone's attention. Thank goodness.

"Why would you tell me something like that?" Aunt Connie asked.

My father shrugged and said, "Cause that's what big brothers do to their little sisters."

"Who then end up inadvertently tormenting their big brother's children!" Aunt Connie shot back.

"Ah, the circle of life," Dad said.

I laughed. "Speaking of little sisters, where's Lizzie?"

"She's with Simon," Aunt Connie said.

"Oh, great!" I said. "She's probably telling him all about the flamingo soup."

"In that case, I'd better get back!" Aunt Connie said with smile. She wrapped her arms around me and whispered, "Hate to say it, Caper, but I think my surprise was better."

She let go and ran back to the restaurant. Mom gave me one of those sideways hugs that seemed to be the way we hugged now that I was getting older.

"Feel like dessert?" she asked.

"If it's all right with you, can we maybe do it someplace else?" I asked. "I don't really want to go back in there. At least not for a couple of years."

We walked to the valet stand, where Dad handed Mom the ticket so she could get the car.

"Well, I suppose I should probably get back in there and pay the bill. Here, Caper." He put his sport coat around my shoulders. I slipped my arms through the sleeves.

"Not a bad fit," he said and then went inside.

"Can you grab my bag, Dad?" I called after him. I noticed Mom looking over my shoulder. She quickly reached down and unfastened the dog collar. She nodded over my shoulder again. I turned around, and there was Serena Kingsley and her family.

Try as I might, I wasn't able to render myself invisible. There was nothing I could do but stand there and smile. Surprisingly, Serena smiled back when she saw me. She said something to her parents and walked over. I took a couple of steps away from Mom, who helped out by stepping back even further.

"You okay, Caper?" Serena asked.

"Yeah," I said. "Just a little...uh..." I was going to make up something diabetes-related but I decided not to. Not to her. "Just a family thing."

Serena nodded, followed by an awkward pause. This day seemed to be filled with them.

"I'm sorry," she said.

I dress up like a dog and cause a scene the likes of which Happy Clammy's has never experienced, and she's sorry? What did Serena Kingsley have to be sorry about?

"I should've told you. I mean I tried, on Thursday at lunch. I really wanted to tell you but I didn't."

I rewound my mental video tape and remembered the odd glances she kept sending me during lunch.

"I should've told you which eighth graders made the poster. It wasn't my brother, I swear, but he knows who did, and I told him he'd better get them to turn themselves in otherwise I'd do it."

"Walker told me he thought his brother was involved," I said.

Serena nodded. "And I also feel bad about what I said in the General Store today."

I could barely keep up. The General Store. Earlier in the day. Something about e-mail. Right, the password thing. Got it!

"No, you were totally right," I said. "What Andy and Walker do is so wrong." I didn't make an attempt to defend myself, because I thought I'd come across as completely lame. Turns out I didn't have to.

"No, I was wrong," she continued. "Jonny e-mailed Skip who told Mary who called and told me the whole story. I shouldn't have assumed that you would do something like that." I was thinking if there was something I needed to apologize for, but all I heard was this little voice calling, "Tell her! Tell her you like her!"

"Okay. Bye, Caper." Serena started to walk back to her parents.

"Hold on, Serena," I said. "I have something for you." I took out my wallet and removed the folded up sticky note. I held it out to her. "Andy and Walker gave it to me to make up for the whole thing with the poster. But I didn't do anything with it. I wouldn't. I swear."

She came back and took it from my hand. She opened it up and laughed.

"Those dorks got the wrong password," she said. She folded it back up and put into her purse. Her parents' car pulled up and she got into the back. Serena opened the rear window.

"Are you going to our party next weekend?" she asked. "I'm sure Mary wouldn't mind if I re-invited you."

"I don't know. I'm…going out to have dessert with my family right now. I'll let you know. Thanks."

Serena smiled back at me as the car pulled out of the parking lot.

"She's very nice," Mom said.

I had to agree.

SUNDAY

The next morning was Hebrew school. It was Jonny's mom's turn to drive, and the whole way there he was dying for me to tell him what had happened. Of course I couldn't say anything with Eric and Shari right there, and there was no time during school that we could sneak away long enough for me to do it justice, so he had to wait until we got home. His mom was willing to drop him off at my house but he would have to walk home from there.

As soon as we got inside, the phone rang. From somewhere in the deepest recesses of the house, Lizzie shrieked, "I GOT IT! I GOT IT!"

Everyone froze. Ever since Mom and Dad gave her phone-answering privileges, the rest of us had learned to stay out of The Lizard's way. She was so excited about getting the phone she even jumped off the toilet once just to answer it. Anyway, we heard the clattering of her footsteps coming up the basement stairs. A double THUD followed by a pathetic YOW and then the basement door flew open so hard the doorknob made a dent in the wall behind it. Lizzie stumbled into the kitchen hunched over with one hand covering what was quickly becoming an enormous bruise on her left shin. She jumped up onto the counter with her one good leg and grabbed the phone just before it rolled over to voice mail.

"Hi!" she yelled into the phone. "Uh, I mean, Speigelman house." As she listened, Lizzie's eyebrows scrunched up. "Who? Oh, yeah. I remember. Phil's fine. Yeah." She put the phone on the counter and limped back to the basement door. "It's for you, Caper." She disappeared downstairs.

"Who is it?" I shouted at her, but she was already gone, her job done. I picked up the phone. "Hello?"

"Hey, Caper, how're you doing? It's Simon."

Oh no! Simon! I wanted to throw the phone down and run away, but I held on. My mind tried to convince me that Simon was calling to tell me that, while he was too much of a gentleman to have said anything last night, he was breaking up with Aunt Connie because there was no way he could date someone with a nephew as immature and thoughtless as me. I must've wandered far off into my mind, because the next thing I heard was, "Caper? You still there?"

"Yeah, sorry," I said. "What's, uh, up?"

"Just wanted to see how you were doing," Simon said.

"Uh, fine."

"Great," he said. "Listen, your aunt tells me that you like basketball. If you're interested, I've got tickets to game six of the playoffs next weekend—if they make it that far."

Simon was asking me to go to a basketball game with him? After how I treated him the night before? I didn't get it, but I also didn't want to look a gift horse in the mouth.

"Sounds great," I said. "But I have to check with my parents."

"Absolutely," Simon said. "Your aunt gave me your e-mail address. I'll send you the info and just get back to me."

"Okay," I said. "Bye. And thanks! Bye."

We hung up and that was that. I told my folks what Simon said and they smiled.

"So, if having our son call him names and having our daughter inundate him with wild stories about flamingoes doesn't scare him off, I guess nothing will," Dad said.

"So I can go?" I asked hopefully.

"Let's see how the next few days unfold," Mom replied.

Jonny and I ran up to my room where I finally began to recount the entire night's proceedings, starting with the gift bag switch when I got home. I paced around my room and, at some point, started re-enacting the whole night, and not just my part either. I lost all track of time and it wasn't until I stopped and looked at the clock that I realized I had been speaking for twenty-nine minutes straight.

Jonny just sat there. I could tell the wheels in his head were turning but I had no idea what he was thinking about. After sitting there speechless for a couple of minutes, Jonny looked me in the eyes.

"She digs you."

That was it? That's what he had to say? Never mind embarrassing myself in front of a crowded restaurant or saying some hateful thing to my aunt's boyfriend or anything like that. Noooooooo! All he could say was, "She digs you."

Jonny checked his watch and jumped up.

"Gotta go, Cape. Have to finish my outline for language arts. See ya tomorrow."

And with that, he left, his sneakers pounding down the stairs. The front door flew open and he was gone.

So that pretty much brings you up to where I am right now. It's Sunday afternoon, Jonny's just left, and I'm still sitting on my bed trying to make sense of what just happened. I mean, here I am, pouring my guts out for the past half hour and my best friend just picks up and leaves me with, "She digs you."

It's like he didn't even hear a word I said about what happened last night! Doesn't he realize that I've been so miserable because I was angry at my diabetes? I was angry about *getting* diabetes, about having to *learn about* diabetes, about having to *live* with diabetes! I got so caught up in thinking about becoming diabetic that I never gave myself a chance to figure out what my feelings were about becoming diabetic.

All this stuff just swimming around inside me until this whole stupid dog thing set me off. The funny thing is that Aunt Connie started it, and I ended up taking all my frustration out on her boyfriend—the only person I've met since I was diagnosed who has any idea what I'm going through.

But does Jonny get any of this? Noooooooooo! All he can say is, "She digs you."

Does he really think that Serena Kingsley "digs" me? Me? Come on! I mean, so what, so she came up to me last night and apologized for accusing me of sneaking into her e-mail. And told me she's going to get those eighth graders to turn themselves in. And of course she didn't say a word about, you know, what everyone else in the restaurant obviously saw. And then, sure, she re-invited me to Mary's party and...wait a second...wait a ding-dong second.

Huh. Maybe Jonny's right. Maybe she digs me.

Hmm. It's kind of weird being dug. In fact, I'm not quite sure I know what to do with that information.

But if there's one thing this week has taught me, it's that I better have a plan.